BERGER AND MITRY
MYSTERY
10

THE
COAL BLACK
ASPHALT TOMB

THE
COAL BLACK
ASPHALT TOMB

A Berger and Mitry Mystery

DAVID
HANDLER

MINOTAUR BOOKS

A THOMAS DUNNE BOOK

NEW YORK

A Thomas Dunne Book for Minotaur Books.
An imprint of St. Martin's Publishing Group.

THE COAL BLACK ASPHALT TOMB. Copyright © 2014 by David Handler. All rights reserved. Printed in the United States of America. For information, address St. Martin's Press, 175 Fifth Avenue, New York, N.Y. 10010.

www.thomasdunnebooks.com
www.minotaurbooks.com

Library of Congress Cataloging-in-Publication Data

Handler, David, 1952–
    The coal black asphalt tomb: a Berger and Mitry mystery / David
Handler. — First ed.
        pages cm.
    ISBN 978-1-250-04197-5 (hardcover)
    ISBN 978-1-4668-3918-2 (e-book)
    1. Berger, Mitch (Fictitious character)—Fiction.   2. Mitry, Desiree
(Fictitious character)—Fiction.   3. Murder—Investigation—Fiction.
4. Mystery fiction. gsafd   I. Title.
    PS3558.A4637C33 2014
    813'.54—dc23

                                                    2013032877

Minotaur books may be purchased for educational, business, or promotional use. For information on bulk purchases, please contact Macmillan Corporate and Premium Sales Department at 1-800-221-7945, extension 5442, or write specialmarkets@macmillan.com.

First Edition: March 2014

10 9 8 7 6 5 4 3 2 1

For Kate Miciak,
who changed Hoag's diapers

The
Coal Black
Asphalt Tomb

CHAPTER 1

Ba-boomp-boom-pah ... Ba-boomp-boom-pah ...

Des still couldn't get used to it as she idled there in front of the firehouse in her Crown Vic, heater blasting on this damp, chilly April morning. She couldn't get used to these privileged, pigment-challenged high school kids blasting gangsta rap on the sound systems of their BMWs and Mini Coopers as they came roaring through the Dorset Street Historic District to school, slowing their preppy selves down to the twenty-five mph speed limit only because they saw her there. How was it possible that these Jennifers and Trevors from the gem of Connecticut's Gold Coast got off on some thug rapper lipping about a life that would totally freak them out if they ever actually experienced it for themselves?

Ba-boomp-boom-pah ... Ba-boomp-boom-pah ...

Dorset's Resident Trooper didn't get it, possibly because she was the only woman of color currently residing in this New England WASP Eden, population seven thousand, at the mouth of the Connecticut River. Then again, maybe if she were ten years younger she'd get it. Instead, these kids made her feel, well, not young. Spring's arrival was doing that to her this year. For the first time in her life, the season of renewal was making her feel, well, not new. Her twenties had started to disappear in her rearview mirror. And on a raw, cold morning like this, she got out of bed feeling what her time on the job had done to her. The ache in her right forearm from when she'd gotten shot with a .38 up at Astrid's Castle. The stiffness in her lower back from that time a crack dealer shoved her down a flight of steps in the Frog Hollow projects. A tightness in her right hamstring for which she had no explanation at all. Face it, her body was not as limber or forgiving as it once was. Not like these teenagers cruising past her.

Ba-boomp-boom-pah . . . Ba-boomp-boom-pah . . .

Not that Des wanted to be sixteen again. She was happy to have left all of that confusion, panic and acne behind. But time kept on slipping, slipping, slipping into the future faster than she cared for. And what did she have to show for it? She'd been a hotshot homicide lieutenant on the Major Crime Squad before she nuked her career and ended up here, busted down to a master sergeant, her prospects for advancement nil. As for her drawings of the murder victims who she'd encountered on the job—the gruesome, luminous art that gave her life purpose and passion—she'd slammed headfirst into a creative wall. Des had been upping her game at the renowned Dorset Academy in her spare time. Or trying to. Had absolutely loved the advanced life drawing class she was taking from an inspiring young teacher named Susan Vail. But a rash of home invasions on Griswold Avenue last month forced her to miss so many studio sessions that she'd had to drop out. And now she could *feel* how her skill set was holding her back. Couldn't get down on paper what she saw in her head. Needed to spend more time drawing and less time idling here watching these kids, and life itself, pass right on by.

Des allowed herself one wistful sigh before she eased her

cruiser out into Dorset Street, with its picture postcard colonial mansions and white picket fences. Her destination was Dorset's stately white-columned Town Hall, where she maintained a cubbyhole and mail slot. From the outside, Town Hall looked the same as it always had. But the old place was totally different inside. The sleepy hush was gone. So was the musty smell. The wall-to-wall carpeting that reeked 365 days a year of mildew, mothballs and Ben Gay had been taken up, the oak plank floors underneath stripped and refinished. Des still wasn't accustomed to hearing the thunk of her polished black size 12½ AA square-toe oxfords as she strode down the hallway to her cubbyhole. But she liked it. She liked the new vibe.

It had finally happened. Dorset had a new leader. And not just any new leader. For the first time in history Dorseteers had elected a living, breathing first selectwoman. Des's snowy-haired nemesis, Bob Paffin, the weak-chinned patrician *noodge* who'd done nothing but disrespect, undermine and hose her ever since she became resident trooper, had finally been unseated after serving Dorset for the past thirty-four years. Bob Paffin had been first selectman for so long that hardly anyone could remember what he used to do for a living. Turned out he'd been in real estate, as in the Paffin family owned a lot of it. Publicly, Des had stayed neutral throughout the campaign. Privately, she was absolutely thrilled that Bob was out.

And Glynis Fairchild-Forniaux was in. Glynis was a pretty little blue-eyed blonde in her late thirties. She and her husband, Andre, Dorset's mobile veterinarian, had three young children together. And Glynis, a tough, savvy graduate of Harvard Law School, had the oldest and bluest of Dorset's blue-blood law practices. Glynis took it over from her late father,

Chase Fairchild. Glynis had represented Des when she bought her house. Des liked Glynis and had long thought she'd make a great first selectwoman.

Not everyone in Dorset had agreed. Her candidacy had been bitterly opposed by the old guard, most notably Clyde "Buzzy" Shaver, who was the editor and publisher of Dorset's weekly newspaper, *The Gazette*. Not to mention Bob Paffin's oldest friend and most ardent backer. In the closing weeks of the campaign Buzzy had blasted Glynis in a front page editorial as "untested, inexperienced and dangerous." To which Glynis had responded, "A radiation spill is dangerous. I'm an attorney, a wife and a mother." When the dust settled Glynis had won by a whopping nine votes. Two recounts had to be held before Bob Paffin finally conceded.

Glynis was someone who cherished Dorset's quaint New England charm. But her election represented a tectonic shift of generational sensibilities in the serene village that Des and the Jewish man in her life, Mitch Berger, a film critic from New York City, now called home. The new first selectwoman had insisted that Dorset needed to modernize its infrastructure so as to be more responsive to the needs of its young families. From now on all public meetings would be available to residents via live podcast on the town's spanking new Web site. From now on, Glynis would post regular video updates and stay in touch with Dorseteers via Twitter and Facebook. Bob Paffin? Bob Paffin thought social networking meant having lunch at the country club every day with Buzzy Shaver and a gaggle of old cronies.

But the first selectwoman's most ambitious undertaking was the historic district's boldest public works project in more than a generation. And one that the old guard was incredibly miffed about. Everybody agreed that Dorset Street needed repaving. It was strewn with boulder-sized potholes and hadn't been re-paved in years. And even that had been merely a resurfacing of the existing road—which was typical of Bob Paffin's penny-pinching stewardship. Not only was the drainage terrible, but Dorset Street still had all of those bumpety-bumps under it from where the old trolley tracks used to be. The entire road-bed needed to be dug up and regraded, Glynis believed. She also wanted to widen Dorset Street so as to accommodate a bike lane. *And* she wanted sidewalks where there were none, most notably where Dorset Street met up with McCurdy Road in front of the steepled white Congregational Church. This meant that three towering Norway maples that had stood in front of the church since forever would have to go.

The old guard was not happy.

Buzzy Shaver, who'd taken to denouncing the project in *The Gazette* as "Queenie's Folly," had labeled the Dorset Street project a "seizure of sovereign land by jackbooted thugs." But no amount of opposition could deter Glynis. Put a wall in front of Dorset's new first selectwoman and she would simply run through it. She had to be the most determined woman Des had ever met.

Town Hall was swarming with computer techies and elec-tricians that morning. In fact, Des discovered an electrician on his knees under the desk in her very own office, with his butt facing the door. Electrician's crack, she decided, was ev-ery bit as uninviting as carpenter's crack. However, the pres-ence of this man and his butt crack meant she would finally have enough outlets in there to power a desktop computer, modem, printer and window air conditioner all at the same time. Imagine that.

As she stood there in the doorway, leafing through her mail and wondering when her right hammy would stop throbbing, Des heard brisk footsteps clack-clacking toward her in the oak-planked hallway. Bob Paffin used to creep around the carpeted hallways, the better to eavesdrop. Not Glynis. You knew she was coming from fifty feet away. And she was always in a hurry—all five-foot-three of her.

"You are *just* the person I wanted to see," she said excitedly, her blue eyes gleaming up, up at Des, who towered over her at six-foot-one. Glynis had a fluty little voice that could lull the unsuspecting into thinking she was an airhead. The unsuspecting soon learned otherwise. She wore a charcoal pants suit with a cream colored silk blouse and pearls. Her hair was gathered back in a tight ponytail. "It's *all* happening, Des. The tree crew will be arriving this morning at ten o'clock sharp to take down those nasty old maples in front of the church. And the people from Wilcox Paving have confirmed that they will *definitely* start the regrading tomorrow at dawn."

Des shoved her heavy horn-rimmed glasses up her nose. "Did you just say tomorrow?"

"This is incredibly short notice," Glynis acknowledged. "But they had another job fall through, their equipment's available and we'll be saving the town nearly two hundred thousand dollars if we squeeze them in now rather than waiting for the peak summer season."

"Which is when our elementary school, middle school and high school aren't all in session," Des pointed out. "Not to mention the Dorset Academy."

"I know it'll be a total traffic nightmare for you. But they've promised me they'll keep one lane of Dorset Street open at all times. And provide their own flagmen. And the weather forecast looks decent. They'll be in and out in three days. We'll e-mail and robo-call every resident in our database to let them know. And I'll need you to kick-start our parking ban. Also our traffic plan. I've just alerted the boys at public works to get all of the barricades ready. They're bitching and moaning like a bunch of old women, I must say."

"Not to worry, they'll deal," Des assured her. "We'll all deal."

"Thank you, Des. I'd be lost without you." Glynis rubbed her small hands together gleefully. "I watched the video of the equipment Wilcox uses. Did you know there are no jackhammers anymore? They have this amazingly huge asphalt grinder that rolls along at the rate of seventy-five feet per minute and *eats* the pavement. Chews it up and spits it out through a conveyer into dump trucks. After the roadbed has been graded and rolled, the trucks feed an equally huge paver thingy that heats up the old pavement and extrudes it smooth as new. They did warn me that the equipment's loud. And I understand it'll make everything shake. But when it's all done Dorset Street will be *beautiful*."

"I'm sure it will."

"The boys at public works can take care of the sidewalks after they're gone."

"I'm sure they can."

"But step one is those darned trees." Glynis puffed out her cheeks. "And you know how irrational some folks can get about such things. Don't get me wrong: I understand about wanting to keep things as they are. But great gosh almighty, we're talking about three half-dead maples, not the lighthouse out on Big Sister. Four different licensed arborists have pronounced them diseased. The darned things are likely to come crashing down on the power lines any day now. They *have* to go. But certain people refuse to face facts." Glynis glanced up and down the hallway, then lowered her voice. "My mother has heard a rumor . . ."

"What kind of rumor?"

"A few of the old-timers are talking about staging an Occupy Wall Street type of protest. Meaning there may be a small, tasteful stink when the tree crew shows up this morning. I need you there in case it gets unruly, Des. Not that I think it will. But I'll feel better if you're there."

"I'll be there. Do you have any idea who's leading the protest?"

"A very good idea. It's Sheila Enman."

"The old schoolteacher?"

"Old battleship is more like it. Apparently, those trees are very special to her. God knows why. She's been telling people that we'll have to remove them over her dead body. Sheila is ninety-four years old. Can't get around without a walker. Can't drive a car. I can't imagine how she'll even get there from her house."

Des showed Glynis her smile. "Oh, I think I have a pretty good idea how."

CHAPTER 2

SCAREEEEEEEE . . .

Mitch had been up since well before dawn in his antique post-and-beam caretaker's cottage out on Big Sister Island. A big fire was roaring in his fieldstone fireplace and at this very moment none other than Mr. James Brown himself was exhorting him to "Get on up" by way of the digitally remastered funk classic "Sex Machine," which Mitch had discovered was absolutely incredible to sit in with on his sky blue Fender Stratocaster with its monster stack of twin reverb amps. Feeling it, bringing it, blasting his riffs off of Bootsy Collins's thudding funkadelic bass.

Eeeee-yahhhhhh . . .

By the time the sun came up Mitch had already devoted thirty minutes to his yoga practice, powered down a bowl of steel-cut oatmeal and watered the tiny green shoots that were germinating in seed trays under the grow light in his bay window. Then he'd polished off one of the two freewheeling essays he wrote every week for the e-zine he'd gone to work for after he'd resigned as lead film critic for what used to be New York's most distinguished newspaper before it was gobbled up by an evil media empire. Today's essay, "The Unbearable Lightness of Spencer Tracy," was a reflection on how it was possible that a man who'd been universally lauded as the greatest actor of his generation, an Oscar nominee for Best Actor a record nine times and back-to-back winner in 1937 and 1938 for *Captains Courageous* and *Boys Town*, didn't happen to be the star of *one* movie that was on anyone's top ten, top twenty or even top fifty list of the greatest English-language movies of all time. Even those fondly remembered comedies Tracy had made with Katharine Hepburn such as *Adam's Rib* and *Pat and Mike* were stale beer compared to the fizzy champagne of *Bringing Up Baby*, the screwball classic she'd made with Cary Grant—who never won an Oscar. Meanwhile Joseph Cotten, who was never even nominated for an Oscar, had starred in two of the greatest movies of all time: *Citizen Kane* and *The Third Man*. And Dana Andrews, no one's idea of an Oscar-caliber talent, had played the male lead in two of Hollywood's most beloved classics: *The Best Years of Our Lives* and *Laura*. So what was the deal? Had Tracy been overrated at the time? Were Cotten and Andrews simply lucky to have landed in such great movies? Or were those movies great because they were in them? For a screening-room rat like Mitch, such questions were a gourmet meal he could feast upon for hours.

Scarreeeeeeee . . .

In the silence after the final emphatic note of "Sex Machine" Mitch heard a thud against his door. Quirt, Mitch's lean, mean outdoor hunter, was announcing his proud return home by banging his hard little head against the door. Mitch opened it and was immensely gratified to find a fresh-killed bunny on the welcome mat, sans head.

"Why, thank you, Quirt," he exclaimed as the cat darted inside to the kibble bowl that he shared with Clemmie, who seldom roamed outside or went after anything more menacing than a dust bunny. "I feel cherished."

Quirt had been bringing Mitch a gift every morning for the past week. April was officially headless-bunny season out on Big Sister Island, the forty wooded acres of Yankee paradise that Mitch was lucky to call home. There were five houses on the island, not counting the old lighthouse—the second oldest in New England—and his own two hundred-year-old post-and-beam caretaker's cottage. The island had its own beach, tennis court and dock. A rickety quarter-mile wooden causeway connected it to the mainland at the Peck's Point Nature Preserve.

Mitch put on a heavy sweater and work boots and went tromping out into the chilly morning fog on burial detail, inhaling the fresh sea air. The deep snow cover from the long, hard winter was gone. The ground had thawed. He could smell the moist, fertile earth. The snowdrops and daffodils were up. The maple trees in the woods were showing their red buds.

By the time he got back to his cottage, Bitsy Peck, his neighbor and garden guru, had arrived with her garden cart laden with cold frames for his seedlings. Bitsy was a round, snub-nosed, bustling little woman in her fifties who had welcomed Mitch from the day he moved out to Big Sister.

"It's time to force your little charges out into the great outdoors," she informed him, standing there in his driveway in her denim overalls, floppy hat and garden clogs. "I've also brought you some extra cabbage seedlings. You need to grow *a lot* of cabbage this year, Mitch. More and more studies are finding that sauerkraut is a powerful natural aphrodisiac."

"And you're telling me this because . . ."

"Des is a big healthy girl. I want you to be able to keep up with her."

"Thank you, Bitsy. I think. But I don't know how to make sauerkraut."

"Not a problem, I can teach you. Believe me, by this fall you'll be pickling like a master."

Bitsy was always happy to share her garden wisdom. Also her insider's knowledge of Dorset. There wasn't anyone or anything she didn't know about. It was the Pecks who'd first settled Dorset way back in the mid-1600s. Bitsy lived alone in her mammoth, natural-shingled house with its turrets and sleeping porches and amazing water views in every direction. Her husband, Redfield, was no longer around. And her daughter, Becca, a recovering heroin addict, had moved out to San Francisco. Mostly, the lady gardened. Hundreds of species of flowers, herbs and vegetables grew in her terraced beds. Gardening kept her sane. Or at least sane by Dorset standards.

"I wanted to ask you something," Mitch said, steering her toward the muddy clearing where he had his picnic table and Adirondack chairs. The soil underneath them had gotten so compacted that grass would no longer grow there. "What would you think about me putting in a patio here?"

"Why, I think it would be wonderful," she exclaimed. "And I have *all* sorts of bluestone left over from the last walkway I put in. It's just taking up space in my barn. I'll bet we can fashion something that'll be just right for you. I'll stop by later this afternoon and we can conversate about it."

"We can what?"

"Conversate."

"Bitsy, that's not a real word."

"It mostly certainly is. Becca uses it in her e-mails to me all of the time."

"That doesn't make it a real word. We *converse*. We don't *conversate*."

Bitsy heaved her chest at him impatiently. "Mitch, we don't have time for this right now. Not if we're going to be there before ten."

He glanced at his watch. "You're right. If I don't pick up my prize package by 9:30, she'll blow a gasket. I'd better scoot."

"Me, too. I've got at least five very anxious people waiting for me at the senior center." She grinned at him conspiratorially. "Why do I feel like we're plotting to overthrow the government?"

Mitch grinned right back at her. "Because we are."

His prize package, a ninety-four-year-old retired high school English teacher named Sheila Enman, lived in the lush farm country north of the village, in an old red mill house that was built right out over the Eight Mile River at the base of a twenty-foot waterfall. Sheila had lived there since she was a little girl. Back in those days they generated their own electricity, she'd once told him. And Sheila had attended an actual one-room schoolhouse.

The morning fog was starting to burn off as Mitch piloted his bulbous kidney-colored 1956 Studebaker pickup up Route 156, two hands on the wheel and one of his new toothpicks parked snugly in the corner of his mouth. Hawks circled lazily overhead. Depending on where his gaze fell it was either winter or spring. The magnolias, weeping cherries and Korean azaleas were already in full bloom while the oaks and birches remained bare and iron gray. The wild blackberry, lilac and forsythia that grew in a tangle alongside of the road had just begun to green up.

When he arrived at the red mill house Mitch found the old white-haired schoolteacher standing in the driveway waiting for him, her knobby, arthritic hands clutching her walker for dear life.

"It's about time you got here," she barked at him fiercely. "I was afraid you weren't going to show up."

"I told you I'd be here, Sheila."

"Mitch, men have been disappointing me for more than eighty years. Forgive me if I got dubious."

He helped her into his truck, depositing her walker and shoulder bag in back. The shoulder bag was extremely heavy. It also clanked when he set it down. He jumped back in and started his way back down Route 156, Sheila riding next to him in her ratty yellow cardigan, dark blue slacks and bone-colored orthopedic shoes.

Sheila was a classic cranky Yankee—feisty, opinionated and stubborn beyond belief. But once Mitch got to know her he discovered that she was a sweetie. And sharp as can be. Age hadn't slowed her mind one bit, just her big-boned body. She'd had a bad hip for years but refused hip replacement surgery. Also refused to abandon her house for an assisted-living facility. Mitch brought her groceries three times a week, picked up her mail at the post office, shoveled her driveway and did odd jobs around the house for her. She paid him with tubs of her homemade tapioca pudding. As far as he was concerned, he was getting the best of the deal.

"I made some calls," he informed her as they drove along. "Channels Three, Four, Eight and Nine."

She looked at him hopefully. "Do you think they'll send someone?"

"I know they will. Local news broadcasts are all about visuals. We're giving them a visual. It's tailor-made for them."

"Good. Because I will not be shoved aside."

"Not to worry, Sheila. You won't be."

She continued to look at him. Or, more specifically, at his new toothpick.

"Something the matter?"

"Why, no," she said. "Nothing at all."

Bitsy beat him there. When Mitch pulled up she and her minivan load of five angry, sign-wielding old ladies were already gathered outside of the Congregational Church holding their SAVE OUR TREES signs. He fetched Sheila's walker and shoulder bag for her and dutifully helped her do what she'd come to do—which was chain and padlock herself to one of the three gnarly old maples out front like a nonagenarian eco-freak, her walker positioned before her for support.

Their timing was excellent. Less than a minute after Mitch had snapped the padlock shut for her, a big bucket truck from Shoreline Tree Service came rolling up, along with a truck towing a wood chipper. Two more vehicles trailed close behind them. One was a town-owned Toyota driven by Dorset's first selectwoman, the other a Crown Vic cruiser piloted by Mitch's ladylove.

"Good morning, Master Sergeant," he said, beaming at her as she strode across the lawn toward him, squaring her big Smokey hat on her head. "Would you slap me down if I mentioned how pert you look today?"

Des narrowed her pale green eyes at him. "Did you just say *pert*? I don't do *pert*. Fluffy little princesses named Amber do. . . ." She trailed off, frowning at his new toothpick.

"Something wrong?"

"Why, no," she replied as the Channel Three news van pulled up. The Channel Eight van was right behind it. "What are *they* doing here?"

"Someone sort of called them."

"Someone sort of media savvy?"

"Sort of."

"Sort of like yourself?"

"Well, yes, now that you mention it."

"Mitch, please tell me why you did this."

"Because Sheila asked me to. What was I going to tell her—no?"

The vans from Channel Four and Channel 9 arrived now. As the news crews got set up, a tall young guy with a camera came out of the offices of *The Gazette*, just down the street, and started taking photographs. What with the half-dozen protestors, Mitch, Bitsy and the guys from the tree crew it was turning into a full-fledged crowd by Dorset standards.

Glynis was not pleased. In fact, the first selectwoman was downright steamed. She marched right over to Sheila and declared, "This won't accomplish a thing, Miss Enman. These trees are diseased and dying. They have to make way."

"I'm diseased and dying, too," Sheila roared in response as

the TV cameras rolled. "Are you going to haul me away, too? And don't you dare lecture me, Glynis. I can still remember you running around at the Memorial Day parade with your diaper full of poop."

"Oh, this isn't getting us *anywhere*," Glynis fumed.

"Perhaps you'd like to take a look at this," Mitch said, offering Glynis the framed black-and-white photograph that could usually be found on Sheila's living room mantel. It was an old photograph of a gawky young girl standing in front of this very Congregational Church with a shovel in her hands and a proud expression on her face.

"Okay, what am I looking at?" Glynis demanded.

"This was taken on Arbor Day, 1931," Mitch explained. "That was the day Sheila personally planted these three trees. It was her prize for winning the Center School essay contest on 'Why I Love Trees.'"

"Sheila *planted* them?" Glynis gasped in disbelief. "Why didn't she tell me?"

"She didn't feel she had to. She thought it was up to you to do your homework. A bit perverse on her part, I'll grant you. But Sheila's getting to be kind of stubborn."

"Sheila's always been stubborn."

"Can't you accommodate her?"

"How, Mitch? Tell me how."

Mitch told her how. Glynis looked at him in astonishment, then gave him a wink and started her way back over to Sheila, who remained padlocked to one of her beloved trees. The news cameras moved in closer.

"Sheila, how would you like to plant the new trees?" Glynis offered.

"*What* new trees?" Sheila demanded, scowling at her.

"The three new trees we'll put in as substitutes for these when we finish the project. You could plant them if you'd like to. Just as you planted these."

"Don't you talk down to me, Glynis."

"You've known me my whole life. Have I ever talked down to you?"

Sheila preferred not to answer that. "What kind of trees?"

"I can't speak for the tree commission," Glynis replied. "But it seems to me we should be able to plant whatever kind you want."

"I want copper beeches," Sheila stated firmly. "No itty-bitty saplings either. Good-sized ones."

"Then I'll propose that we install good-sized copper beeches. Would you like that, Sheila?"

Sheila Enman stuck out her chin and responded, "I'll think it over."

"Boyfriend, have you ever thought about going into politics?"

They were lolling in his bathtub sipping Chianti while the pancetta and onion caramelized on low heat in his cast iron skillet and *Workingman's Dead* played on the stereo. The master sergeant's slender right ankle was hoisted up on his left shoulder so that he could massage her hamstring, which had been troubling her lately.

"Why are you asking?"

"Because you handled that situation with Sheila Enman

this morning like a pro. First you invented a crisis for the news cameras . . ."

"I thought you looked mighty delectable on Channel Three, by the way."

"All you could see of me on Channel Three was my booty."

"Like I said, I thought you looked extremely delectable."

"*Then* you helped solve the crisis. Face it, you're a natural politician."

"Am not. I was just trying to mollify the old girl. She's deeply invested in this place emotionally. Glynis doesn't seem to get that."

"She's a bit focused," Des acknowledged. "You could help her out."

"How?"

"By serving on a commission. She's desperate for young voices. Did you know that the average age of Dorset's commissioners is seventy-three?"

"Des, I'm a journalist. We don't do things like serve on commissions."

"What *do* you do?"

"Sit back and criticize the people who do. Besides, I already work at the food pantry. I deliver groceries. I drive folks to their doctor appointments. And those town government meetings are *excruciatingly* slow. If I want to be that bored for that many hours I'll sit through a Terrence Malick film." He set down his wine glass and reached for a fresh toothpick, popping it into the corner of his mouth.

She peered at him critically. "Okay, what's with this toothpick deal?"

"Actually, it's not a 'toothpick' at all. That's the beauty of it. It's a Stim-U-Dent plaque remover. Cleans between my teeth *and* gently invigorates my gums while also giving me a certain Cagney-esque jauntiness. It's a win-win, don't you think?"

"What I think is that you're going to swallow it and I'll have to rush you to Shoreline Clinic. What brought this on?"

"I went to the dentist when I was in the city last week, remember? When he got done examining me I asked him if I had any cavities. Know what he said? He said, 'At your age cavities are no longer your biggest concern.' Then he told me my gums are receding and if I don't start taking better care of them all of my teeth will fall out. I mean, God, what's up with that?"

"We're becoming middle-aged, wow man. Get used to it."

"I don't want to get used to it. Do you know that rather powerful, goaty scent that a lot of the old men in Dorset give off?"

She nodded. "Only too well."

"If I ever start to smell like that will you kindly shoot me?"

"It'll be my pleasure."

"Thank you. You're very kind." He went back to work on her hamstring, kneading the taut tendon, flexing her foot to stretch it out. "Feel any better?"

"A bit," she acknowledged. "But I'm still not looking forward to tomorrow. Eating road dust from dawn until dusk is not what I want to be doing at this stage of my life."

"What do you want to be doing?"

She lay there in silence for a moment. "I don't know the answer to that. I used to, but now I don't."

Mitch studied her, frowning. Something had been eating

at her for a while. He had a pretty good idea what, but he also knew that she'd only open up about it when she was good and ready to. That was her way. So he didn't press her. Instead, he ditched his toothpick, leaned over and planted a kiss on her mouth.

Her eyes gleamed at him. "What was that for?"

"I was just remembering how lucky I am to have you in my life."

"Right back at you, boyfriend."

"Hmm . . . I think my onions are overheating."

Now she was looking at him through her eyelashes. "Is that some kind of Jewish-boy dirty talk?"

"No, it's our dinner starting to scorch," he said, sniffing at the air. "I'd better check on it."

"Be with you in a sec. I'm going to wash my hair."

He dried off, put on a pair of sweatpants and his New York Giants hoodie and padded into the kitchen to take a spatula to the onions and pancetta before they burned. He hadn't known for sure if Des would be joining him for dinner. But he was totally cool with their arrangement, which was loose, spontaneous and cautious. Even though they were deliriously happy together they were taking it a day at a time as their wounds slowly healed. Des was still getting over her brutal divorce from that cheating louse Brandon. And Mitch had barely survived losing his wife, Maisie, a Harvard-trained landscape architect, to ovarian cancer at the age of thirty. Both of them needed their own living spaces so they could do what they did in private to cope. Des got up before dawn and drew haunting, viscerally horrifying portraits of murder victims. Mitch? He often sat up all night long watching old movies, sometimes four or five of them at a stretch, losing himself in his comforting alternate universe where good was good, bad was bad and everything turned out like it was supposed to in the end. He and Des enjoyed the time they spent together and enjoyed the time they spent apart. They didn't dwell on how unlikely a couple they were. And they for damned sure didn't sweat small stuff like dinner. Mitch kept a few key ingredients on hand so he could put together a tasty meal at a moment's notice. Tonight he would throw linguine into the skillet with the onions and pancetta, break a couple of farm-fresh organic eggs over it and toss it with a ton of grated aged Parmesan, chopped Italian parsley and fresh ground pepper. There was crusty bread, a bottle of Chianti Classico. What more did they need?

He set the table in the living room while Des showered. It was a drop-leaf table that he'd found discarded in one of his neighbor's barns along with two moth-eaten overstuffed chairs and a loveseat. Clemmie was parked in one of the overstuffed chairs. Quirt was outside looking to bite the head off something small and furry.

Mitch was putting another log on the fire when there was a tap at his front door. "Come on in!" he called out.

It was Bitsy—and she wasn't alone. Standing there in the doorway with her was a tall, lanky woman in her seventies named Helen Weidler. Helen was a highly efficient legal secretary who'd gone to work for the first selectwoman's father, Chase Fairchild, way back when she was in her twenties. Worked for him until he retired, then stayed on when Glynis took over the practice. Helen was still at Fairchild & Fairchild, making sure things ran smoothly.

"How nice to see you again, Helen." Mitch knew her because Glynis had handled the closing on his house, same as she'd handled Des's. "Won't you ladies come in?"

Bitsy made her way straight for the seed trays in Mitch's bay window, the better to inspect his tiny green shoots. Helen hovered close to the door, wringing her hands and looking exceedingly tense. Her attire suggested she'd come straight from the office. She wore a matching dark gray sweater and slacks, a white blouse and polished black pumps. Helen's hair was white and she wore it cropped in that severe light-bulb shaped cut that, for reasons beyond Mitch's comprehension, was favored by many women of her age in Dorset. Helen had a long narrow face and a mouthful of rather prominent teeth. She'd never married, as far as Mitch knew.

Des joined them now, wearing the dove gray four-ply cashmere robe Mitch had bought her in Paris.

"Oh, dear, we're interrupting your evening," Bitsy said fretfully.

"Not at all," Mitch assured them.

"As long as you don't mind seeing me out of uniform," Des agreed as she settled into an overstuffed chair, curling her long legs beneath her

Helen remained anchored by the doorway, glancing around the room. Mitch's desk was an old mahogany door he'd scored at the dump and set atop a pair of sawhorses. His coffee table was an old rowboat with a storm window over it. There were books and DVDs heaped everywhere. Clutter was a constant presence in his life. "So this is where you live," she observed. "It's very cozy and charming. Mind you, I've always believed that the ambiance of a home is a reflection of the people who live in it, as opposed to the furniture or the artwork." She cleared her throat. "I apologize for barging in this way."

"Not to worry," he said. "Bitsy and I are practically like family. And so are you, Helen. I would never have survived the closing on this place if it hadn't been for you. Chances are I'd still be hyperventilating in the parking lot outside out of the bank. You're the one who came out and dragged me inside to sign the mortgage papers. Do you remember what you told me?"

She frowned at him. "Why no, I don't."

"You said, 'Grow a pair, will you?' Those words meant a lot to me, Helen. Please have a seat here by the fire. Can I pour you ladies some wine?"

"You talked me into it," Bitsy said brightly.

"I'm not much of a drinker." Helen perched hesitantly on the edge of the sofa next to Bitsy. "But do you have any Scotch?"

"A very nice Balvenie. How do you take it?"

Helen blinked at him. "In a glass."

He went into the kitchen and turned off their dinner. Fetched the bottle of single malt Scotch from the cupboard and poured Helen a generous jolt. Then filled a glass with Chianti for Bitsy and returned to the living room.

Helen swallowed her entire glass of Scotch in one gulp, shuddering. "Thank you, Mitch. I needed that. Warms you right down to your toes, doesn't it?"

"Yes, it does. Would you care for another?"

"I believe I would."

He refilled it for her. This time she took only a small sip, her hand trembling as she clutched the glass.

Mitch picked up Clemmie and sat down in the chair she'd occupied, settling her in his lap. He sipped his wine. He waited in patient silence.

"Please don't tell her I've come here," Helen finally blurted out.

"By 'her' do you mean Glynis?"

Helen nodded. "I have to tell you something very, very important. If Glynis digs up Dorset Street tomorrow morning this town will be torn to pieces and no one will ever be able to put it back together again. Do you understand me? No one."

"Have you spoken to Glynis about this?" Des asked her calmly.

Helen looked down into her glass. "I can't speak to her about it."

"Why not?"

Helen didn't respond, just sat there in tight-lipped silence.

"Why can't Glynis tear up Dorset Street?" Des pressed her.

"Because some things . . ." Helen took another small sip of her Scotch, gazing into the fire. "Some things are better off left as they are. I was hoping and praying that it wouldn't come to this, you know. That Bob Paffin would win the recount. That Glynis wouldn't be able to push through her plan. Why does she have to be so darned good at what she does? Why couldn't she just be another ineffectual dodo bird like Bob Paffin?" Helen looked at Des imploringly. "*Please* make sure that they don't dig up Dorset Street tomorrow morning."

Des glanced helplessly over at Mitch.

He cleared his throat and dove in. "Why can't they dig it up?"

"It's needed regrading for years and years. Haven't you folks ever wondered why the work was never done? Why they just kept resurfacing it?"

"I figured that Bob didn't want to spend the money," Des said. "He was Mr. Small Government."

"A total cheapskate," Helen acknowledged with a curled lip. "But that's not the real reason."

"Helen, what are you trying to tell us?" Des wondered. "Is something *buried* underneath the pavement?"

Helen didn't answer her. Just stared into the fire, her jaw muscles tightening.

"Do you know what this is about?" Mitch asked Bitsy.

"I know that Helen's not kidding around," Bitsy replied. "She means what she says. And there's good reason to believe her. I've been hearing about this ever since I was a little girl."

"Hearing about what?"

Now it was Bitsy's turn to stare into the fire. "It isn't talked about."

"*What* isn't?" Des demanded. "With all due respect, ladies, you're both talking in riddles. I have no idea what you're getting at. And even if I did there's absolutely nothing I can do at this point. The town has already advanced Wilcox Paving a nonrefundable deposit. The crew will be arriving at the staging area in less than ten hours. I can't help you."

Helen bit her lip in anguish. "You have to, Des. Please stop it."

"I can't, Helen."

The old secretary lowered her eyes, crestfallen. "Of course not. I understand. Well, that's that. I've said what I needed to say. I told myself I had to do that much or I wouldn't be able to sleep tonight. Just remember that I warned you, okay?" She finished off her Scotch and got to her feet. "We've taken up enough of their time, Bitsy. They need to eat their dinner and do all of the other wonderful things that young couples do on a raw evening when there's a fire going and a bottle of wine open." And with that Helen marched out the door and was gone.

"Sorry for dumping this on you," Bitsy said. "But she's an old friend and she was so insistent. Thank you. Both of you." And then she scurried out the door after Helen.

Mitch headed into the kitchen to turn the burners back on under the skillet and pasta water. "What on earth was *that*?" he demanded. "Wait, wait, my bad. This one's in your wheelhouse. You should go first."

"Thanks, don't mind if I do." Des joined him in the kitchen, wine glass in hand. "What on earth was *that*?"

"If I didn't know better I'd say Helen's no longer getting an adequate blood supply to her brain."

"But we do know better. Helen's a practical, hard-nosed woman who's been a trusted legal secretary to the Fairchilds for her entire adult life. Cuckoo she's not, agreed?"

"Agreed. That was one genuinely frightened woman. Whatever Helen's freaked out about is real. And it sounds like she's been sitting on it for a long, long time." He stirred the pancetta and onion as it began to sizzle again. "What are you going to do?"

"There's nothing I can do. I don't have the authority to halt the dig at the very last minute. Only Glynis can do that. It would cost the town a boatload of money and there's absolutely no way she'll agree to do it based on a cryptic warning from her own damned secretary who, for reasons known only to Helen, won't speak directly to Glynis about it." Des shook her head. "What does Helen think I can do? Why did she even come here?"

"She told you—so she could sleep tonight."

"Well, I'm glad. That makes one of us."

The pasta water came back to a boil. Mitch dumped the linguine in, stirred it and set the timer. Then he started chopping the parsley.

"Mitch, I have a very stupid question for you."

"It's your lucky night. I happen to specialize in very stupid answers."

"Have you seen this movie before?"

He thought it over before he nodded his head.

"So tell me."

"Tell you what, Des?"

"What's Helen so afraid of? What's down there?"

"It's not a what," he said quietly. "It's a who."

CHAPTER 3

IT TURNED OUT DES was wrong. There was no road dust at all. Just a whole lot of damp, compacted soil that reeked of creosote. The oily smell hung heavy in the air. After a while she swore it had seeped into her skin.

The morning was clear and frosty. It was supposed to climb into the upper forties by the afternoon. No rain in the forecast today. A mere 30 percent chance of a few showers tomorrow, which was about as good as a forecast could get this time of year in southern New England.

Work began two hours before daylight. That was when the Wilcox Paving crew came rumbling into town like an invading army, with a convoy of flatbeds, dump trucks and water trucks. There were at least a dozen men on the crew, not counting the foreman and flagmen. Their staging area was the parking lot of the A&P on Big Branch Road, which was the only space big enough for them to off-load their immense equipment from the flatbeds. Des was there to greet them as they rolled in. They were a quiet, highly efficient bunch. The husky young foreman had everything under control. Mostly, Des stood there chugalugging coffee and trying to wake up. She hadn't slept well. Not after Helen Weidler's tangled-up-in-weird warning.

At 5:15 AM the first selectwoman made a personal appearance at the staging area—in the flesh *and* in costume. Glynis wore an orange safety vest over her charcoal gray pantsuit, a pair of tan work boots and a shiny white hard hat.

"Welcome to Dorset, gentlemen!" she said excitedly as she tromped around shaking hands with each and every crewman. "Good morning, Des! This is going to be a great day, isn't it?"

"Yes, it is. What's up with the hard hat?"

Glynis furrowed her brow. "Why, think it's too much?"

"No, no. It's always good to be prepared. But what are you preparing for?"

"I'm thinking it will mollify the angry soccer moms if I stand out in front of Center School myself. If they want to bitch about the traffic they can bitch at me, not you."

"Well, I'm all for that. Just please do me one small favor, will you?"

"Sure, Des. What is it?"

"Don't get run over. My troop commander would never forgive me."

The mandatory parking ban on Dorset Street was scheduled to go into effect at 6 AM. Des got in her cruiser and made a circuit of the historic district to make sure that each and every resident had complied. If they hadn't, their vehicle would be towed immediately to the impound lot in Westbrook.

But things looked good, she observed, as she swung slowly through the district in the predawn darkness. The barricades and safety cones were in place. And the parked cars were gone. It was all good.

Make that *almost* all good.

At the corner of Dorset Street and Appleby Lane there was still one car parked at the curb in front of the public library. It was a black Volvo 850 station wagon, a well-worn model from the late nineties. It was a popular car around Dorset, where people held on to their cars for a long, long time. There were still dozens of black 850s around. She had no idea whose this one was until she ran the plate—and discovered to her great displeasure that it belonged to Buzzy Shaver, editor and publisher of *The Gazette* and the road project's most vociferous opponent. Des wasn't sure if this was Buzzy's idea of a one-vehicle protest or what. But his car wasn't parked anywhere near the office of *The Gazette*, which had been headquartered a mile down Dorset Street since 1926. And the old curmudgeon's house was situated at least a half mile down Appleby Lane from the library. She could think of no reason why his car was parked here.

Other than to mess up the first selectwoman's pet project, that is.

Des reached for her cell and woke him up. Or it sure sounded that way.

"Wha' . . ." he demanded hoarsely.

"Mr. Shaver, this is Resident Trooper Mitry. You need to move your vehicle immediately."

Buzzy Shaver's response was a nasty, phlegmy coughing fit that went on for quite some time. After that all she heard was wheezing.

"Mr. Shaver, are you still there?"

"Of course I am," he growled. "But why are you bothering me at this ungodly hour?"

"Because you are currently in violation of a mandatory parking ban. If you don't move your vehicle at once I will have it towed at your expense."

He wheezed at her some more before he said, "Our *fee-male* first selectman put you up to this, didn't she?"

"The clock's ticking, Mr. Shaver. Would you like me to come get you or can you make it here on foot?"

"Don't talk down to me, young lady," he blustered, slamming the phone down.

It took him ten minutes to make his way down Appleby Lane on foot, gasping and wheezing. He'd thrown on a buffalo plaid wool shirt, baggy slacks and an old pair of Bass Weejun loafers. Buzzy Shaver was a lifelong bachelor well into his seventies and not exactly any woman's idea of eye candy. He had a loose, pendulous lower lip and a mouth full of rotting yellow teeth. His face sagged into a diverse community of jowls, wattles and dewlaps, and his bald head was mottled with liver spots. His shoulders were soft and round, and the man had almost no neck. Des thought he looked like a turtle. An angry turtle.

"I don't see why you had to make such a fuss," he grumbled at her. His eyes were bloodshot, and his breath was foul enough to make her knees buckle.

"That makes us even, Mr. Shaver. I don't see why you chose to ignore a mandatory parking ban."

"Young lady, I don't particularly care for your tone of voice."

"And I don't particularly care for you holding up progress this way."

"I'm doing nothing of the sort."

"Really? Then why isn't your car parked in your garage?"

"That," he replied, "is none of your damned business."

"You made it my business, Mr. Shaver. I'm authorized to tow it and stick you with the bill. I extended you a courtesy by phoning you. Now show me some courtesy in return or so help me I will write you out a ticket, understand?"

"All right, all right. Don't get your panties in a twist."

"I'm sorry, *what* did you just say to me?"

Buzzy Shaver got into his Volvo and started it up. "Here's a piece of advice," he offered as he rolled down the window. "You'll get along a lot better in Dorset if you do something about your hostile attitude."

Des smiled at him through her gritted teeth. "Thank you for sharing that with me, Mr. Shaver. I'm so appreciative."

And so proud of her self control. She did not—repeat, not—discharge her firearm into the old man's car as he drove away.

After that, things proceeded quite smoothly. The mammoth asphalt grinder left the staging area on schedule and at precisely 6 AM began eating its way through one of Dorset Street's two lanes and conveying the chewed up pavement to the dump trucks that trailed along behind it. The entire historic district did shake, rattle and roll. But all that was left in the grinder's wake was bare soil and that aroma of creosote. The road grader that followed the grinder smoothed the dirt with its huge blade, then a water truck wetted it down and a roller readied it for repaving. The operation was choreographed for maximum efficiency. Not a moment was wasted.

No question, the morning school traffic was a nightmare

to funnel in and out with only a single lane open. But Des had the assistance of another state trooper in uniform and two Wilcox Paving flagmen. And the first selectwoman's own buoyant presence out there in her orange safety reflector and hard hat did keep Dorset's busy moms from freaking out over being stuck in standstill traffic.

By the time the morning rush hour was over the big asphalt grinder had already gobbled its way past Town Hall. Glynis took off her road-crew costume and resumed normal activities in her office. Des got in her cruiser, circled her way around the historic district and pulled onto the shoulder of McCurdy Road next to the barricade they'd set up there. By now the grinder was nearing the Congregational Church. Just past the church, where Dorset Street made a sharp left at McCurdy, the grinder was supposed to swing around and begin chewing its way back up the other side of Dorset Street.

That never happened.

It had just eaten up the pavement in front of the church when all hell broke loose by the road grader that was trailing along behind. Des could hear crewmen hollering and whooping as the grader came to an abrupt halt and then backed up. The caravan stopped. The operators jumped out of their heavy machines and convened in the middle of the road. One of the flagmen waved his arms frantically at Des. She hopped out and hurried toward them.

What she saw when she got there had to qualify as the weirdest sight she'd encountered in her entire career.

The grader's blade had exposed a shallow grave right there in the middle of the road, underneath the pavement. A human body in full US Navy dress blues was buried there. Had been for a long, long time. The remains were skeletal. Some strands of mouse-colored hair still clung to the skull. The wool material of the dress uniform was rotted but recognizable. So were the two stripes on the shoulders and sleeves as well as the corroded gold-plated pin on the dead lieutenant's chest. Des, who'd graduated from West Point, recognized it as a gold wings pin. Its wearer had been a Navy flyer.

"Not something you see every day," the husky young foreman said to her hoarsely.

"No, it is not." Now Des noticed that the grader's operator was sprawled on the ground in front of his machine, bleeding from the forehead. He looked dazed. "What happened to your man?"

"He fainted and hit his head," the flagman told her.

Des immediately placed a call to Madge and Mary Jewett, the no-nonsense fifty-something sisters who ran Dorset's volunteer EMT service. Then she asked the trooper who was helping with traffic flow to secure the perimeter and keep absolutely everyone away from the grave—particularly the tall young blond guy who'd just moseyed over from *The Gazette* and was trying to take pictures. She darted back to her cruiser for her own Nikon D80 so she could zoom in for a better look at the body without touching it or compromising the gravesite.

The lieutenant's shirt, tie, shoes and socks had decomposed, she observed as she snapped pics. His toe bones were exposed. Around the bone of his left wrist he wore a wristwatch that appeared to be a stainless steel Rolex Submariner.

Its band of stainless steel links was intact. Around the bones of his right ring finger he wore a ring. Mighty bulky one. Mighty dirty, too. But Des thought it looked like a service academy class ring. It had a reddish birthstone set in the middle of it. Possibly a ruby. Hard to say for sure. She saw nothing else that might offer a hint to the lieutenant's identity. And it was not, repeat not, her job to search his remains for identification.

By now the Jewett sisters had arrived. Mary got busy checking out the dazed operator of the grader.

Madge stared down at the skeletal remains and shook her head in wonderment. "Good gravy, it's *him*. I always thought it was one of those made-up legends, like Bigfoot or trickle down economics. Tell me, are those gold wings he's wearing?"

"Yes," Des said.

"Then it must be him."

"Must be who, Madge?"

Madge blinked at her. "Lance Paffin, of course. Who else could it be?"

"Would Lance Paffin be any relation to . . ."

"He was Bob's big brother. A hotshot Navy flyboy and major heartthrob, I'm told. Before my time." Madge gazed at her curiously. "I keep forgetting how new you are to this place. You've never heard about Lance?"

"This is what I'm saying."

"After a big night of partying at the country club's spring dance in, let's see, this was way back in 1967, I think, Lance took his catboat out for a moonlight sail. His boat was found washed up on the rocks at Saybrook Point the next morning. The Coast Guard searched and searched but his body was never found. There's a headstone in Duck River Cemetery bearing his name except . . ."

"Except what, Madge?"

"Well, there's always been this legend that he *didn't* wash out to sea. That something else happened to him."

"Such as what?"

"Des, what in the heck is he doing underneath Dorset Street?"

"Kind of wondering that myself." Des turned to the foreman and said, "I'm afraid that all work will have to be halted until further notice. This is now a crime scene." She would have to notify Glynis of this as well. But first Des placed a direct call to her troop commander in Westbrook, a grumpy, sagging accordion of a man who absolutely hated to rub up against anything high profile, controversial or stressful. Something told her that this one was going to qualify as all three. When he answered she took a deep breath and said the words that she knew he wouldn't want to hear. She said, "Captain Rundle, this is Master Sergeant Mitry. Sir, we've got something just a tiny bit unusual here."

It took the vans from the medical examiner's team forty minutes to get there from Farmington. There were five people in all—a team leader and four worker bees. The chief medical examiner arrived in a separate car to take charge of the scene personally, which was something he almost never did. His being there set off alarm bells in Des's head. Clearly, she was experiencing a close encounter of the skunky kind.

Des was by no means idle while she waited for them to arrive. Captain Rundle sent her two more uniformed troopers to help her reroute all traffic from the area and keep the local TV news camera crews and lookie-looks away. She obtained contact information for all of the crewmen who'd witnessed the unearthing of the shallow grave. She also notified Glynis and asked her to search the town's public works records to determine the exact date when Dorset Street had last been regraded. It took Glynis less than ten minutes to supply the answer, thanks to her recently mandated conversion of Dorset's musty files to computer discs. The last time Dorset Street had been stripped down to the bare soil was a major regrading project that took place between the 16th and 24th of May, 1967.

Glynis delivered this information to Des in person at the site. She wanted to see it for herself. Stayed there with a stricken expression on her face, her mouth scrunched tight as she watched the medical examiner's team carefully remove the skeletal remains on a plywood board so that no bones would be lost.

But no matter how careful they were, Des knew they'd erect a tent around the grave site and undertake a painstakingly thorough archeological dig, sifting and screening every bit of the compacted soil, digging inch by inch with their tiny tools and brushes so as to make absolutely, positively certain that no bones, personal effects or pieces of crime-scene evidence were left behind.

Meanwhile, she expected the Major Crime Squad to arrive any minute now to take charge of the criminal investigation into the death of this Navy flyer who'd been buried under Dorset Street for the past forty-seven years. Because there was no doubt that a crime had taken place. Otherwise, hello, he wouldn't be under Dorset Street, would he? All of which meant the first selectwoman's signature road project would have to be put on hold for days. The crew from Wilcox Paving would no doubt pack up their massive equipment and leave for another job. And God only knew when they'd come back. Glynis was not happy.

Nor was Captain Rundle. He'd listened in dread-filled silence when Des filled him in on the phone. After she'd finished laying out the highly speculative ID scenario regarding Lt. Lance Paffin he told her go about her business and await further instructions from him.

When he called her back Rundle said, "Master Sergeant, you'll have to take charge of this one yourself for now." He cleared his throat. "It seems that all three of our Major Crime Squads are up to their ears. They've got a rape homicide, a home invasion double homicide and a gang-related shooting. Those take priority over some old skeleton. It's not as if he's going anywhere, right?" She didn't hear dread coming from him now. She heard fear. Her guess? He'd just gotten leaned on big time. And she had a pretty damned good idea by whom. What she didn't know was why. He cleared his throat again. "Besides, the last thing we want to do is raise any red flags. We'll have the FBI and NCIS crawling all over this, and we don't want that, do we? So it's your case for the next day or two. God knows you have the experience. I'll keep major crimes in the loop. As soon as a team frees up you'll hand off, got it?"

"Yes, sir."

"As far as the media goes, just tell them we've found some unidentified remains that may or may not be human. You have nothing further to say. If they want more details refer them to our public information officer in Meriden."

"Yes, sir."

"And tell those men on the paving crew to keep their mouths shut. We don't want them blabbing about what they saw on TV. Same goes for the EMT people."

"Sir, the first selectwoman has just passed me some interesting information. The last time Dorset Street was regraded was back in May of 1967. That coincides with when Navy Lieutenant Paffin disappeared at sea, I'm told."

Rundle fell silent.

Stayed silent for so long that she finally said, "Sir? . . ."

"Pursue this matter discreetly. I am talking kid gloves. Keep thorough documentation. And if you have any questions I want you to contact me personally. No one else. At some point later today you'll be . . . just wait for further instructions, okay?"

Translation: She would not know what in the hell was going on until a certain higher-up got in personal touch with her and told her what in the hell was going on. That certain higher-up being the imposing ramrod of a deputy superintendent who everyone in the Connecticut State Police called the Deacon.

And whom she called Daddy.

The Cyrus Paffin House was a barn-red saltbox-style colonial that had been built in 1732, according to the quaint little historic plaque next to its front door. It had been home to generations of Paffins ever since, as had the twenty acres of prime Frederick Lane real estate that surrounded it. Frederick Lane, which forked off of the Old Boston Post Road about a mile north of the historic district, was considered one of the choicest addresses in Dorset. Some of the finest old homes in town could be found there.

Former First Selectman Bob Paffin and his wife, Delia, had spent most of their married life in the old Cyrus Paffin house. Their eldest son, Harrison, now lived there with his wife and children. Bob and Delia lived in a newer place on the same property that you didn't know was there unless you knew it was there. Des had learned that this was typical of the Dorset blue bloods. The older the money the harder it was to find.

A pair of smooth, well-tended gravel driveways adjoined the old saltbox. One driveway led to a garage and garden shed out back. The other driveway, which was the one that Des took, snaked its way past the garage and through the woods that were behind it. From the street it appeared as if there was nothing but woods all of the way down to the banks of the Lieutenant River. Appearances were deceiving. The gravel driveway eventually reached a three-acre clearing where a snug, natural-shingled cottage with blue trim overlooked the tranquil river. Bob and Delia had designed and built the cottage for their retirement. It was very private, very peaceful, very nice.

Des parked her cruiser in the driveway and got out, hearing nothing but the chirping of the birds and the crunch of her footsteps on the gravel. She rang the doorbell. She waited.

It was Delia who answered the door, accompanied by an ancient, arthritic white toy poodle that barked at Des without much conviction.

Des tipped her hat politely. "Good morning, Delia."

Delia responded by staring at her in clench-jawed silence. Everyone in Dorset professed to adore the former first selectman's wife. She served on the board of directors of the Dorset Day Care Center, the Youth Services Bureau, the Welcome Wagon and a gazillion other worthy local institutions. Des often heard her referred to as a "treasure" and a "dear." In fact, Des had never run into anyone who didn't go out of their way to say how warm and giving Delia was. Des wouldn't know about that. Delia Paffin had never given her anything but the big chill from the day she arrived.

"Why, Resident Trooper Mitry," she said finally, her eyes glinting at Des from the doorway. "To what do we owe this honor?"

"I'm sorry to intrude on you folks. Just wondered if I could have a minute of your time. Bob's time, actually."

Delia frowned at her. "I'll have to see if Bob's free. Would you care to come in?"

Des stepped into the entry hall, which was furnished in a vaguely Danish-modern style and reeked of one of those pine forest-scented plug-in thingies that Des detested. Made your whole damned house smell like a highway rest stop lavatory.

"I apologize for the odor," Delia said, managing a tight smile that did not reach all of the way to her eyes. "I'm afraid we have a choice of either deodorizer or pee-pee. Poor old Skippy can't control himself like he used to."

Poor old Skippy was sniffing at Des's ankles. Smelled her cats no doubt. Des watched him, wondering if he was going to hoist his leg and let her have it.

Delia watched the dog, too, possibly hoping he would. She was a plump, apple-cheeked dowager with a head of carefully sculpted hair that was dyed a most peculiar yellowish orange. The only other time Des had seen that same exact color it was inside of a blue box of Kraft Macaroni & Cheese. Des supposed that Delia had been attractive when she was young if a man's taste ran to the ample milkmaid type. She was not someone who'd ever been delicately proportioned. Not with those meaty wrists and hands. She was dressed in a cream-colored turtleneck sweater, dark brown slacks and pearls.

"I'll see if I can find Bob," she said.

"No need to search around." Bob Paffin came strolling in from the sunroom. "I'm right here."

Skippy let out another half-hearted bark.

"Atta boy," Bob said to him. "You keep right on protecting the fort."

Dorset's recently ousted first selectman of thirty-four years was red nosed, snowy haired and weak chinned. He was a thinly built man, not particularly tall. Des guessed that Delia outweighed him by a solid thirty pounds. He had on a white button-down shirt, tan crew neck sweater and gray flannel trousers. He didn't appear to be any happier to see Des than Delia was—for the simple reason that he wasn't. He'd never liked anything about Des. Not her skin color. Not her gender. Not the way she went about her job. Not one thing.

"How are you, Bob?"

He answered with a shrug of his narrow shoulders. "Well enough. Haven't the slightest idea what to do with myself all day long but that's my problem, not yours. What can I do for you?"

"We've had a bit of a situation with the dig."

"Of course you have. That's what happens with these big government projects. They're taxpayer-funded disasters. That's why I always opposed them. Buzzy Shaver phoned me ten minutes ago and told me."

"Told you what?"

"That the whole darned operation had come grinding to a halt."

"Did he tell you why?"

"He didn't have to. There's always a foul-up."

"Bob, I'm about to say something that you may find disturbing. I suggest you sit down."

He crossed his arms in front of his chest, staring at her defiantly. "I'll stand on my own two feet if you don't mind."

"As you wish. I understand that you had an older brother, Lance, a US Navy flyer who disappeared off of his sailboat in Long Island Sound one night."

"That's right," Bob said grudgingly. "He took the *Monster* out and never came back. That was ages ago. Way back in '67."

"Do you remember the exact date?"

"Of course I do. It was the twentieth of May. Why?"

"According to town records, Dorset Street was in the process of being regraded the night he disappeared. In fact, that's the last time it was regraded."

"So? . . ."

"So I'm here to inform you that the paving crew just uncovered the skeletal remains of a US Navy flyer in dress blues buried in a shallow grave under Dorset Street. There's a distinct possibility that the remains are those of your brother Lance."

Bob Paffin gaped at her in goggle-eyed shock before his legs gave way underneath him. Des caught him by the armpits as he started to crumple to the tile floor. She hoisted him over onto a small bench next to the front door.

"How dare you?" Delia's eyes blazed at Des angrily. "My husband has a heart condition."

"I did urge him to sit down," Des said as Bob slumped there, stunned.

Delia rushed into the kitchen and returned with a bottle of Courvoisier and a glass. She filled the glass and held it out to him.

He took it from her and gulped it down, shuddering slightly. Then he sat there breathing slowly in and out. "I'm . . . okay now. I'm fine. Just don't do well with shock. Never have. I-I guess you'd like to talk about this."

Des nodded. "If you're up to it."

He handed the empty glass to his wife and stood back up. He seemed steady enough on his feet. "Of course. Come on in."

There was a round glass table in the sunroom where it looked as if Bob and Delia had been playing a game of gin rummy. Delia wiped the cards from the table and the three of them sat down there, Skippy settling himself at Delia's feet.

From where she sat Des could see a long, long way up and

down the Lieutenant River. "This is a lovely spot," she observed, acutely aware that Delia hadn't offered her coffee. A minor social slight, but Des noticed it. She was meant to. This was how disses were served in Dorset.

Bob was gazing across the table at her in disbelief. "This must be some kind of a sick joke. Are you telling us that my brother has been underneath Dorset Street this whole time?"

"I'm telling you that *someone* has been under Dorset Street. And absolutely no one is regarding it as a joke, sick or otherwise. The chief medical examiner has attended the site personally. And the officer's remains are being treated with the utmost care and respect."

"Well, do you know *how* he died?"

"Not yet. We won't know until the ME conducts a thorough examination. And it may be impossible to tell after so many years."

"But you . . . you think it's Lance?"

"That's what I'm here to find out. We need your help, Bob."

"Of course. Anything I can do."

"Anything," Delia chimed in. "Anything at all."

Des reached for her notepad and pen. "For starters, would you happen to remember how tall your brother was?"

"Lance was an honest six-footer, unlike a lot of men who claim to be but are actually five-foot-ten."

"Do you recall if he had any distinguishing injuries?"

Bob looked at Des blankly. "What are those?"

"Did he suffer any broken bones when he was growing up?"

"He did, yes. Lance broke his collarbone sledding down Johnny Cake Hill when he was, oh, ten years old."

"Right or left?"

"Right, I'm pretty sure. And he broke his left wrist playing basketball in high school. Some thug from Old Saybrook tripped him."

"Did Lance wear jewelry of any kind?"

"His naval academy class ring. Never took it off. He was so proud of it. Remember, Delia?"

"I remember," she said quietly.

"Which finger did he wear it on?"

"His right ring finger." Bob narrowed his gaze at her. "Did you recover his ring?"

"What month of the year was Lance born?"

"July."

"That would make his birthstone . . ."

"His ring had a ruby set in it."

"And he was a member of which class?"

"The class of '62. His class motto was the word 'honor.' It was engraved on the ring. And his name was engraved on the inside. "

"Did Lance wear a wristwatch?"

"Yes, he did. Our folks gave him a Rolex Submariner as a graduation present."

"Which wrist did he wear it on?"

"His left." Bob ran a bony hand through his white hair. "This kind of information will help you figure out whether or not it's Lance?"

"It'll help. Were you and Lance full brothers?"

"What on earth does that mean?"

"Did you share the same biological mother and father?"

"Of course we did," he said indignantly. "Why wouldn't we? He was born six years before I was. It was just we two. Mother was unable to have any more children after I was born."

"Bob, I'm sorry for the inconvenience but a technician from the ME's office will probably stop by later today to take a cheek swab from you."

"What on earth for?" Delia demanded.

"If Bob and Lance were full brothers then Bob's DNA will match that of the remains."

The Paffins both fell into horrified silence.

"I-I just don't understand how this is possible," Bob said.

"That's what we're going to find out. I've been asked to get some background about the night your brother disappeared. Can you tell me about it?"

"It was the night of the spring dance at the club. A Saturday night. The twentieth of May, as I said. The spring dance was a serious event back in those days. It marked the official launch of the social calendar. That meant brand new gowns for the ladies. White dinner jackets for the gents. A full orchestra, dancing, prime rib, champagne."

"Sounds like fun."

"It *was* fun," Delia acknowledged, thawing one, possibly two degrees. "I may be a bit biased but I believe we had a lot more fun in those days than the young people do now. Boys were boys. Girls were girls. And all of us were young and foolish."

Out on the river a snowy egret swooped low over the water as it flew upriver, flapping its wings effortlessly.

"Lance attended the dance?"

"Yes, he did," Bob replied.

"In his dress blues?"

Bob nodded. "He was home on leave for a couple of weeks from Vietnam. Scheduled to go back the very next morning, in fact. I attended the dance with this lovely young lady right here. I'd recently asked Delia to be my wife and she had accepted. I graduated from Brown the year prior to that. Got my real estate license and went to work in the family business."

"You didn't serve during the Vietnam War?"

Bob colored slightly. "Couldn't. I have a slight heart murmur. I've had it my whole life. It doesn't really give me any trouble."

"It most certainly does," Delia clucked at him.

"But nothing could hold Lance back. My big brother had as sharp a mind as you'll ever come across. He got accepted to Yale *and* Harvard. Instead, he chose Annapolis. He wanted to serve. Lance was . . ." Bob broke off, gazing down at his hands. "I was always in awe of him. He was a strapping, handsome fellow who was so full of life that he lit up the room. Men were drawn to him. He was a natural leader. And the girls were helpless around him. One spin around the dance floor was all it took. My brother had star quality. I'm positive that he would have achieved great success in politics, business—any career that he chose. When he died the best of us died. Would you care to see his picture?"

"Yes, I would."

He got up from the table and led Des into his study, a wood-paneled lair lined with bookcases. Delia followed the two of them in there. She was not about to leave Bob alone with the resident trooper. Nor was Skippy. It was carpeted in there, which meant it smelled even stronger of dog pee and Glade. There was an executive-sized walnut desk. Comfortable leather armchairs. And many, many framed photos on the wall of Bob and his big brother Lance. Bob had been a scrawny youth with a big Adam's apple and a frightened look on his face. Lance had been muscular and quite handsome, if your taste ran to rugged Adonis types with strong jaws and confident grins. He wore his uniform so well that he looked like a damned recruiting poster. One of the pictures was of him hard at work sanding a single mast wood-hulled catboat.

"That's the *Monster*," Bob said, his gaze following hers. "She was a little honey. Lance named her after the golden retriever we had when we were kids. He loved that boat. She was a twelve-and-half-foot Herreshoff that was built back in '39. He bought her for a song while he was in high school and restored her all by himself. Are you familiar with the Herreshoff, Des?"

"Afraid not," she said.

"It was designed by Nathanael G. Herreshoff way back in 1914 as a training boat for young sailors in Buzzards Bay. It has a heavy keel and is stable in gusty conditions. Lance loved to sail her. That's when he was at his happiest." Bob's face fell. "He took her out that night after the dance. I never saw him again."

"Did Lance come to the dance with a date?"

"By himself. He wasn't seeing anyone special. He joined us at our table for a while. Lance was always welcome to join us if he cared to, although he wasn't really part of our group. We were a younger bunch. A nice little group of friends who'd all grown up together. There was Delia and me. There was my oldest and best school chum, Chase Fairchild, our first select-woman's father. My God, it's been seven years now since Chase passed away. I still can't believe he's gone. He was fit as a fiddle. Played tennis three times a week. Then one day the doctor told him he had pancreatic cancer and in a couple of months he-he was gone. Just like that." Bob broke off, his eyes moistening. "Chase was in a particularly giddy mood the night of the spring dance. He'd worked up the nerve to pro-pose to Beryl Beckwith, the girl who would become Glynis's mother. That took nerve, believe me. Beryl was *the* prettiest girl in town."

"She's still a lovely woman," Delia pointed out. "And I swear she hasn't gained a single ounce since college."

"Every guy in Dorset wanted to marry Beryl," Bob re-called. "Except for me, of course. I'd already met my dream girl."

"Now don't be silly," Delia chided him. "I was never in Beryl's league."

"Who else belonged to this little group of yours?"

Bob lifted his weak chin slightly. "Luke Cahoon, naturally. Luke and I have been pals since we were in kindergarten."

Okay, now it made sense. Now Des knew why she'd heard fear in Captain Rundle's voice on the phone. Pennington Lucas Cahoon had been Southeastern Connecticut's repre-sentative to the US Congress for the past forty years. Luke

Cahoon was a fixture on the nation's political stage—an outspoken, independent-minded blue blood whose family had called Dorset home for more than three hundred years. The Cahoons were one of the first families that had settled in Dorset. The congressman still maintained the historic white colonial that he grew up in at the top of Johnny Cake Hill Road. A caretaker looked after the place. A caretaker and Des. When she first became resident trooper it was made crystal clear to her that she was to drive by the congressman's house every single day and check its doors and windows. Mostly, Luke Cahoon was a creature of Capitol Hill, where he claimed that he voted his conscience, not his party affiliation. Which happened to be Republican. This made him something of a relic. He was one of the only moderate social progressives who still sat on the GOP side of the aisle. Possibly the only one. But Luke Cahoon was so popular with voters of both parties that no one ever bothered to mount a serious campaign against him.

"Mind you, he was still just plain old Luke back in those days," Bob pointed out. "Still had two more years of law school to go at Yale because he'd taken time out to serve as a US Marine in Vietnam. Luke's a decorated war hero, as you may know. But by the time he got home from there he was so fervently against the war that he became the leader of Yale's antiwar movement. That's how he ended up in politics." Bob's face tightened. "He and Lance didn't agree about the war at all. They argued about it constantly."

"Did they argue about it the night of the spring dance?"

Bob nodded. "Every time they saw each other. Political

passions ran high in those days, Des. People were involved. They cared. These days they don't care as much about anything, except possibly the outcome of *American Idol*. It's kind of a shame, if you ask me."

"That was the night Luke met Noelle, wasn't it, Bob?" Delia said.

"Yes, I believe it was. Chase and Beryl arranged it. Beryl knew Noelle from Miss Porter's and invited her to join us. Luke had been . . . on his own for a while," he explained. Or, make that, didn't explain. "Noelle Crawford. She was a tall, slim girl with black hair and pale skin. A striking girl. The two of them ended up getting married. They had a daughter together, Katie. But the marriage didn't take. They split up after three years. Luke never did remarry."

"Noelle ended up with an orthopedic surgeon from Marblehead," Delia said. "They were happy together. She's gone now, too. A lot of old friends are."

"And how about Mr. Shaver? Was he part of your group that night?"

"Buzzy and I have been pals our whole lives," Bob replied, smiling faintly. "We were a couple of little stinkers together. Got into all kinds of trouble. But he didn't mix with our group socially. Couldn't. He had to look after his mom. She was very fragile emotionally."

"So your group that evening consisted of three couples plus Lance?"

"That's right."

"It was a lovely evening," Delia recalled in a lilting voice. "Naturally, because of what happened, it's not an evening that any of us can look back on fondly. But we had a lot of fun. We laughed. We drank. We danced out on the terrace. A warm breeze was blowing. The Flower Moon was nearly full."

"Lance was as high-spirited as I'd ever seen him," Bob added wistfully. "He didn't want his last night of freedom to end. Kept insisting we drink one more bottle of champagne, then another. It was way past midnight by the time we cleared out. Everyone else had gone home by then, including the club's staff. And Lance *still* wasn't ready to call it a night. Decided he just *had* to take the *Monster* out for a moonlight sail. One last sail before he returned to active duty. He was . . . what was that word he used, Delia? *Stoked*. He was *stoked* to take her out. He asked us to join him. She held four people comfortably. But no one else was in the mood."

"Not even you?"

"If you knew me better, Des, you'd know that I get seasick in a bathtub. I never go sailing or fishing with anyone."

"The rest of us simply wanted to go home to bed," Delia said.

"So he took her out by himself. And we never saw him again."

"Were you the last people to see him alive?"

"Yes, we believe so. There was no one at the yacht club at that hour."

"And was it you who reported him missing?"

Bob nodded. "He didn't come back. Didn't report for duty in the morning when he was supposed to. I was shocked. But I figured, okay, maybe he fell asleep out there. He did have a lot to drink. Once he's slept it off he'll be back. This is Lance we're talking about. Lance knows what he's doing. I kept checking at the yacht club all day long to see if the *Monster* was back in her slip. His Mustang was in the parking lot. Unlocked, keys in the ignition. It was a white GT. Had the biggest engine they made in those days. Lance loved that car. Loved speed. When he . . ." Bob trailed off, swallowing. "When he didn't come back by late afternoon I called the Coast Guard. They found the *Monster* smashed up on the rocks by the Saybrook Point lighthouse. No sign of Lance."

"Did she have running lights?"

"No, she didn't. But that never stopped Lance. Not when the moon was bright. This was a man who could land a fighter jet on the deck of an aircraft carrier." He gazed out the window at the river for a moment, lost in his memories. "We never knew what happened—whether he lost his balance and fell overboard or what. The only thing I can tell you for certain is that I've never, ever forgiven myself. If I'd gone with him he'd still be alive today."

"You don't know that, dear," Delia said soothingly.

"The Connecticut River was still swollen from the spring rains," he went on. "The Coast Guard figured its current must have washed him out to sea. They combed the North Shore of Long Island and Fishers Island for days, but there was no sign of Lance. And that was that, aside from the nasty whispering, of course."

"What kind of nasty whispering, Bob?"

"Awful stuff. Reprehensible, really. Some folks around Dorset actually believed he'd staged his own disappearance so he could get out of fulfilling his military service. That he was, in fact, sipping tall drinks on an island in the Bahamas with some gorgeous, leggy babe. Garbage. It was slanderous garbage.

I said so at the time to anyone who mentioned it. Offered to punch a few noses, too. My brother considered it an honor to serve his country. Besides, he *loved* that damned boat. He could never, ever have wrecked her on purpose." Bob let out a slow sigh. "Seven years later he was declared legally dead, and a tombstone bearing his name was placed in our family plot in Duck River Cemetery. That's the whole sad story. Or at least I thought it was until you rang our doorbell. Now I don't know a damned thing. Des, what in the name of hell would my brother's body be doing *underneath* Dorset Street?"

Des paused to put on her kid gloves. "With all due respect," she said carefully, "I get the impression that there's some sort of a legend surrounding Lance's death. And not the one you just mentioned."

'They're called *legends* for a reason," Delia informed her icily. "Because they're baloney."

"Baloney," Bob echoed angrily.

"Again, with all due respect, if you folks can shed any new light on this situation it would be greatly appreciated. If, say, something happened that you failed to mention to the authorities at the time—for whatever reason. We sure could use the help now."

Bob and Delia Paffin both stared at her in stunned disbelief. Outside, a squadron of geese flew low over the house, honking loudly. After that it fell silent in the study.

"Let's speak plainly here, Des," Bob said, struggling to maintain his composure. "I know that you and I haven't always seen eye to eye on certain matters. And maybe some of that has been my fault. I'm kind of set in my ways. The voters in town might even go so far as to say I'm an old fool. Fifty-

one percent of them would anyhow. But I want you to promise me something. Will you do that for me?"

"If I can, Bob."

"I want you to find out what in the hell really happened to
my brother."

Des shoved her heavy horn-rimmed glasses up her nose
and said, "Count on it."

CHAPTER 4

"OKAY, I GIVE UP—HOW did you know that it was a *who* buried under Dorset Street?"

"Simple," Mitch said into his cell phone, gasping slightly. He was groping around up in his cramped attic crawl space above the kitchen for Maisie's portfolio. Shortly before she died Mitch's wife had designed an incredible bluestone patio for a garden on West Twelfth Street. "Because of the way Helen was behaving last night. If it had been a *what*—like, say, a chest full of gold doubloons—she'd have been excited. She wasn't. She was frightened."

"Rundle's asked me to take the lead on the investigation for now."

"Oh, yeah? Why's that?"

"Because all three of our Major Crime Squad units are tied up with priority cases."

"Do you think that's the real reason?"

"You know as much as I do. Will you do me a favor? Talk to Helen again. See if she'll tell you why she was so frightened."

"Does this mean you're deputizing me?"

"Baby, you know that only happens in westerns and bad vigilante movies."

"You say that as if there's such a thing as a good vigilante movie. I mean, let's face it, you've got your *Death Wish* franchise, your *Billy Jack* . . ."

"This is strictly unofficial, okay?"

"Well, do we at least get to synchronize our watches?"

"Mitch . . ."

"Righto. Flextime it is. Not to worry, boss. I am on the case."

And now he was steering his high-riding Studey truck back up to Sheila Enman's house, where he'd arranged to run into Bitsy and her friend Helen Weidler while Helen was on her lunch break from the law offices of Fairchild & Fairchild. Helen had been one of Sheila's prize pupils back when Sheila taught English at the high school. The two had remained lifelong friends.

Bitsy's minivan was already parked there when Mitch pulled up at the red mill house that faced the roaring waterfall. He didn't knock on Sheila's door. No point in knocking. Sheila wouldn't hear it over the roar of the waterfall. Since the mill house was built right out over the racing water its first floor tended to get a bit sloshy when the heavy rains came. This had happened twice so far since Mitch had known her. So Sheila had no rugs or upholstered furniture downstairs. Just bare wood flooring and tables and chairs that were practically Shaker in their simplicity. In the kitchen, Helen's stove, refrigerator and washer-dryer were parked on four-inch risers. So was the furnace in her mudroom.

Mitch found the three ladies setting the pine kitchen table with good china, silver and linen napkins. *Ironed* linen napkins. Lunch was a stack of sandwiches made from Sheila's awesome homemade deviled ham on slices of her equally awesome Pullman white bread. There was also potato salad and a bowl of her bread-and-butter pickles if anyone was interested. Mitch was very interested.

"I see that Desiree has talked you out of that dumb toothpick," the ancient schoolteacher said to him in lieu of hello.

"Not at all, Sheila. I've simply changed my mind."

Sheila let out a bray of a laugh. "Of course you have."

Bitsy greeted him with a warm smile. Helen hung back, saying nothing, still extremely ill at ease.

"Have a seat and dig in," Sheila commanded them.

They had a seat and dug in.

As Mitch wolfed down what he hoped would be the first of many deviled ham sandwiches he reflected on the unexpected turn his life had taken since he'd moved to Dorset. Who would have thought that he'd be engineering a secret powwow with three older ladies like this? As he took a sip of milk Mitch realized something even more amazing. Seated here in Sheila Enman's kitchen with the waterfall roaring outside he was somewhere he'd never been before—ground zero of a genuine Dorset gossip mill. He was *at the table.* He savored the significance of this moment before he reached for another half sandwich and said, "Helen, did you know that Lance Paffin was buried down there? Was that why you came to my house last night?"

Helen chewed quietly on a bite of her sandwich, swallowing it. "So they've found him."

"They haven't made a positive identification, but they believe it's Lance. They're keeping a tight lid on it, so please don't mention this to anyone, okay?"

"Whatever is said at my table stays at my table," Sheila assured him.

Bitsy nodded in agreement. "Where was he, Mitch?"

"Right in front of the Congo church."

"Well, that figures," Helen murmured.

"It does? Why's that?"

"Mitch, I came here because Bitsy thought it would be a good idea." Helen's eyes were fastened on her plate. "But I've said too much already."

Sheila let out another laugh. "You are one heck of a tactful person, Helen. I'm not, so I guess that leaves it up to me. Mitch, I can guarantee you that your lady friend will be hearing all about what a war hero Lance was. Which I'm not knocking. If a man serves his country he has a right to be saluted. But there was more to Lance Paffin than that. Much more."

Mitch speared a pickle slice from the bowl. "Such as? . . ."

"Such as that he was the meanest, most vile user of women that it has ever been my misfortune to encounter," Sheila replied. "He wanted them all. And he had them all. Lance Paffin was a predator who had no conscience when it came to women. None. The man was *detested* in Dorset. Believe me, there were dozens of husbands, boyfriends, fathers and sons who would have gladly done him in."

"Helen, how did you know he was down there?" Mitch asked.

"I've . . . heard things over the years," she answered reluctantly. "There's the Missy Lay legend, for one. Not that anyone ever believed a word Missy said. She was an old, old spinster who lived right across Dorset Street from the church. My mother was town nurse back then and got to know her pretty well."

"Goodness, I haven't thought about Missy Lay in years,"

Sheila said with a twinkle in her eye. "The high school kids used to call her Miss Laid. She was a complete loon."

"Missy was *different*," Helen allowed. "My mother told me she used to consume eight fluid ounces of her own urine every single day. Missy believed that it promoted good health."

"And did it?" Mitch asked.

"Well, she lived to be a hundred and three." Helen leaned forward over the table, blushing slightly. "There was also some talk about those fudge brownies that Missy put out for the kids on Halloween."

Bitsy stared at her. "Wait, you don't mean . . ."

"I do," Helen said. "I most certainly do."

Sheila got up and made her way over to the stove with her walker to put the kettle on. "Which explains why no one ever believed anything Missy said."

"What did she say about the night that Lance Paffin disappeared?" Mitch asked.

Helen patted her mouth with her ironed linen napkin before she replied, "Dorset Street had been all dug up. It was a dirt road, and closed to through traffic. No one drove in or out unless they lived in the historic district. So it was very, very quiet outside of Missy's house that night. And Missy, who had terrible insomnia, swore to my mother that she heard men with shovels digging out in the road in the middle of the night. Also that she saw Lance's white Mustang parked there in the moonlight. She told my mother all about it the next morning. Told anyone who'd listen to her after Lance was reported missing. But everyone ignored her because they thought she was potty."

"You believe she really witnessed something, don't you?"

Helen nodded her head. "Because of something I heard for myself at the office one day. Or I should say overheard."

"When was this?"

"About twenty years ago. The last time that Dorset Street was being worked on."

"And what did you . . ."

"My employer, Mr. Fairchild, was speaking to First Selectman Paffin on the telephone. And I heard him say, 'Not to worry, Bob, all they're doing is resurfacing. They won't go down far enough to find anything.'" Helen paused, shaking her head. "I tell you, it made my blood turn cold."

"So you think Chase Fairchild and Bob Paffin knew that Lance was down there?"

"I don't think it. I know it."

Mitch sat there taking this in while Sheila filled a tea ball with multiple spoonfuls of Earl Gray and poured boiling water into her battered silver teapot. Bitsy got up and cleared their empty plates from the table.

"There's fresh-baked cookies in the bread box," Sheila said.

"What a good idea." Mitch fetched them, studying Helen curiously. "Did you tell anyone about this at the time?"

"No, of course not."

"Why not?"

"Why not?" Helen gazed out the kitchen window at the waterfall. "Because Mr. Fairchild would have fired me, that's why not. The day he took me on he told me, 'Helen, from now on you are my confidential secretary. That means anything you see or hear in this office is confidential. If you ever break this confidence I will see to it that you never work in a law office again. Do you understand?' Believe me, I understood.

And I kept my mouth shut. Had to. It was a high-paying job and my situation was bad enough already. I was not exactly the daintiest, loveliest young thing in Dorset. I was a horse-faced goony bird who hadn't been on a date with a man in ten years."

"Don't talk nonsense," Sheila barked at her. "You were a beautiful girl. You had a lovely smile and you were always impeccably groomed. So many of the other girls weren't. And these girls who I see around the village now, my goodness, they're just plain greasy." She turned a frosty gaze on Mitch. "I blame those Hollywood actresses of yours."

"Sheila, are you going to start in on Mila Kunis again?"

"Tell me, does that young woman *ever* wash her hair?"

"I really have no idea. But I'll try to find out if you'd like."

Sheila glared at him. "Are you *humoring* me?"

"Wouldn't dream of it."

"The truth is . . ." Helen shifted uncomfortably in her chair. "I didn't want to go through the rest of my life being mentioned in the same breath as Missy Lay. Everyone calling me a loon behind my back. Besides, no one would have believed me anyway."

"Yet you've decided to speak up now. How come?"

"Because I don't care what people think of me anymore," she answered defiantly.

"That's the single best thing about getting on in years," Sheila said, nodding her head sagely.

"Helen, what about Buzzy Shaver? Did he know, too?"

She frowned at him. "What makes you ask that?"

"He bitterly opposed this regrading project in the pages of *The Gazette*."

"That's because Bob did," Bitsy sniffed. "Buzzy is Bob's toady."

"He also tried to gum up the works this morning."

Bitsy's eyes gleamed at him. "Really? Do tell."

"He defied the parking ban and left his Volvo parked overnight in front of the library. Des had to call him at 6 AM to get him move it. She said he was really rude to her."

"He's a nasty old man," Bitsy said. "But there *is* another explanation. For why Buzzy left his car there overnight, I mean. Hard as I find that to believe."

"I'll say," Helen agreed.

"Okay, I'm not following you."

"Buzzy lives on Appleby Lane," Bitsy explained. "It's a dead-end road. The neighbors are right on top of each other and extremely nosy. Buzzy's a bachelor who visits a lady friend on a regular basis and doesn't wish to advertise it to his neighbors. If he came driving home in the wee hours every night one of them would hear him pulling into his garage. Word would get out that he's seeing someone. So he leaves his car parked on Dorset Street and retrieves it early in the morning. Probably parks down the block from his lady friend's house as well."

"Common practice, Mitch," Sheila said. "Everyone knows that."

"Really? I didn't."

"That's because you live on an island," Helen said. "And you're not a cheat."

"If you were we wouldn't be talking to you," Bitsy said.

"Because Des would have shot you by now," Sheila added.

All three ladies broke out into gales of laughter.

Mitch helped himself to one of Sheila's chocolate chip

cookies, glad he could bring so much mirth into their lives. "Any idea who Buzzy's getting busy with?"

"At his age I wouldn't exactly call it getting busy," Bitsy responded. "It's more along the lines of heavy leaning."

"So whom is he leaning into heavily?"

"Beryl Fairchild."

"Our first selectwoman's mother?"

Bitsy nodded. "He visits her regularly at her little place on Bone Mill Road. Or so I've heard."

"As have I," Helen said.

Sheila made a face. "Why would Beryl keep company with *Buzzy*?"

"Chase has been gone a long time," Helen said. "She's lonely."

"I could never be that lonely," Sheila assured them. "The man is a creep. Always sucking away on that horrible pipe. And that lower lip of his looks like a hunk of raw liver. Can you imagine *kissing* Buzzy?"

Bitsy shuddered. "I'd rather not."

"He doesn't smoke his pipe anymore," Helen informed them. "Had to give it up. He has emphysema. I hear the prognosis is not good."

"Well, I'm sorry to hear that," Sheila said. "But he's still a creep."

She poured their tea now and put out milk and sugar. Mitch tasted his and discovered it was strong enough to dissolve the enamel on his teeth.

He added some milk and said, "Was Buzzy ever married?"

Sheila shook her head. "He stayed 100-percent loyal to mama his whole life. He was absolutely devoted to her. Gladys

Shaver was an emotionally frail woman. Especially after Buzzy's younger sister, Frances, passed away. That was a tragic thing. Buzzy stayed right there in the house with Gladys until she died, oh, four years ago. And he still lives there."

"You make him sound like Norman Bates. Say, he's not into taxidermy, is he?"

"Actually, I always wondered if . . ." Helen cleared her throat. "I thought that he might be more interested in men than women."

"He's a mama's boy," Sheila sniffed. "I'll bet you a shiny quarter that Buzzy's never had sex with anyone in his life, man or woman."

"How did his sister die?" Mitch asked.

Sheila let out a sigh. "Now we're back to talking about Lance again."

"And about me," Helen said, her lower lip trembling slightly.

"Really?" Mitch peered at her. "How so?"

"I had a—a personal experience of my own with Lance," she confessed uncomfortably. "It's not something that I like to talk about. In fact, I've never told anyone about this. . . ."

Sheila reached over and put her knuckly hand over Helen's. "You're among friends, dear."

Helen took a swallow of her tea. "I was at the spring dance myself. The night that Lance disappeared, I mean."

"You attended the dance?"

"Hardly, Mitch. I waited tables there to put myself through secretarial school. My sort doesn't get invited to the club. I'm Swamp Yankee through and through. And not ashamed to say it."

"Nor should you be," Sheila said.

"Lance Paffin was the most gorgeous man I'd ever met," Helen recalled in a small, quiet voice. "As handsome as a movie star. He and I . . . got involved the year before he disappeared. The gang was throwing a birthday party for Beryl Beckwith at the club one night. I was out behind the kitchen on my break, having a cigarette and resting my sore feet, when suddenly Lance was standing there in that beautiful uniform of his, talking to me. When Lance smiled at me I—I just got tingly all over. He made me feel like I was the girl who I'd always wanted to be. There's this dream you've been holding inside since you were seven years old. The one where Prince Charming comes along and rescues you from your life of drudgery. Lance made that dream *real*. It sounds silly, I know. But I was so naïve. He asked me to go for a drive with him after I clocked out. He drove us down to the beach and before you can say *boo* he had me out of my knickers right there on a blanket. It was my first time. Lance was my first." Helen trailed off, her chest rising and falling. "Afterward, he invited me to sail to Block Island with him in the morning. He wanted *me* to spend the whole weekend with him on board the *Monster*. It was all so magical that I floated home on a cloud. Packed my things in the morning and hurried on down to the yacht club. He had told me he wanted to cast off by nine. When I got there he—he had another girl on board. She was as shocked to see me as I was to see her. Lance was shocked, too. Or he pretended to be. Said he was sorry if I'd gotten the wrong impression but that he'd just been kidding around last night. Believe me, he wasn't kidding around when he coaxed me out of my panties. I—I'd never been so humiliated in my life. Went slinking home and cried for two straight days."

Bitsy looked at her in horror. "Helen, I can't believe he did that to you."

"I never got over it," Helen confessed. "I should have, but I couldn't. The next time a young man took an interest in me I was immediately on the defensive. I didn't want to get hurt that way again. It became a—a pattern with me after that when it came to young men. Which isn't to say there were very many. And it wasn't long before they stopped showing any interest in me at all." She swallowed, her eyes glistening behind her wire-framed glasses. "After that I took to watching him in morbid fascination when he showed up at the club dances. There was nothing subtle about Lance. He was relentless. And *so* persuasive. That man could talk proper married ladies into slipping out to the parking lot for a quickie between dinner and dessert. And their husbands never suspected a thing."

"He had his way with more than a few married women," Sheila confirmed. "But his favorite prey was the girlfriends of his friends."

"Not to mention his own brother's," Helen added, nodding.

"Wait, wait. Are you saying he had an affair with Delia?"

Helen arched an eyebrow at Mitch. "If you can call a few quickies in the backseat of his Mustang an affair. Delia was mad for Lance."

"Delia was mad for a lot of the boys," Sheila pointed out. "She was a giggly little pushover in those days, especially if she had a couple of drinks in her. Easy Deezy, they used to call her. She must have had sex with half of the eligible young men in Dorset before she settled on dull-as-dishwater Bob."

Mitch drank his high-octane tea, trying to picture a hefty dowager such as Delia Paffin having furtive parking-lot sex with her future husband's big brother. He couldn't. Maybe because this was the real world, Dorset style. And the real world, he was discovering, was a whole lot sleazier and crazier than anything that Hollywood could dream up. "Did Bob know about Delia and Lance?"

"I'd be willing to bet you that same shiny quarter the thought never so much as crossed Bob's mind," Sheila answered. "Unlike his pal Chase."

Mitch peered at her. "So our first selectwoman's mother had a fling with Lance, too?"

"That's not all she had," Helen said.

Bitsy let out a gasp. "So it's *true*? I've never known whether to believe that story about Beryl or not."

"Wait, what story?" Mitch wanted to know.

"Lance got Beryl pregnant a year before she married Chase," Sheila informed him. "Mind you, Beryl was a much, much steeper hill for Lance to climb. Mount Kilimanjaro compared to Delia. Beryl was a poised, elegant young lady. Well bred, well mannered and *the* prettiest girl in Dorset."

"All of us envied her," Helen said. "Resented her, too. She was *so* perfect."

Sheila nodded. "A man like Lance Paffin couldn't resist her. And she couldn't resist him, apparently. Because it sure wasn't Chase who knocked her up when she was a senior at Wellesley."

"How do you know that?" Mitch asked.

"If it had been Chase's baby they'd have moved up their wedding date," the old schoolteacher explained. "But they didn't. Instead, Beryl went to Barbados for spring break."

"None of that crowd went to Barbados," Helen informed

Mitch. "Hobe Sound was their place. The only reason to go to Barbados was because of a certain doctor who practiced a certain kind of medicine there."

Mitch helped himself to another cookie. "And Chase knew about this?"

"Chase Fairchild was no fool," Sheila said. "But he adored Beryl and he stuck by her."

"How about Glynis? Does she know?"

Sheila considered this, her deeply lined brow furrowing. "I doubt it. That's not the sort of a thing a mother tells her daughter."

"And yet *you* know."

"We do. But we keep our secrets to ourselves. The only reason we're telling you this is because something quite extraordinary happened today. And because we trust you to share it with Des and Des only."

"Thank you for your confidence, Sheila." Mitch nibbled on his cookie in thoughtful silence before he said, "Helen, who was the other girl?"

Helen looked at him blankly. "What other girl?"

"The girl Lance had on board the *Monster* with him that morning."

"Oh. . . ." She cleared her throat uncomfortably. "It was Frances Shaver, Buzzy's kid sister. And I was shocked to see Frances there, believe me, because she was engaged to marry Luke Cahoon at the time."

"*The* Luke Cahoon?"

Helen nodded. "She and Luke were childhood sweethearts. Frances was a lovely, sensitive girl. And the poor thing was easy prey for Lance. She fell hard for him. Hard enough

71

to go sneaking off to Block Island with him behind Luke's back. When they got home Lance tossed her aside—same as he did me."

"Frances was *so* ashamed," Sheila recalled, her face darkening. "She couldn't face Luke after that. She felt she'd destroyed any chance for happiness that they had together. Broke off their engagement and went into a complete emotional tailspin. Ended up taking her life a few weeks later. She slit her wrists. It was Buzzy who found her in the bathtub. She'd locked the door. He had to break it down. It was an awful, awful thing. Gladys Shaver was never the same after that. Nor was Luke. Frances was the love of his life. And Lance just used her and discarded her. Lance Paffin *killed* Frances Shaver. He didn't care about her one bit. The only reason he went after her was to provoke Luke."

"Why would he want to do that, Sheila?"

"He and Luke despised each other's politics. Luke came back from Vietnam an outspoken opponent of the war. Lance was very gung ho."

"The two of them used to get into raging arguments at the club," Helen recalled. "They had one the very night Lance disappeared. Things got so heated between them that Luke challenged him to step out into the parking lot."

"And did they? . . ."

"No, Lance just laughed him off," Helen replied. "Same as he laughed off everything. When I clocked out that night Lance was still sitting with the gang at their table, drinking and having a fine old time. Most of the staff had gone home by then. It was late. But it wasn't unusual for members to stick around and close up themselves. It was *their* club. They stayed as late as they wanted to."

"I'm confused about something, Helen. Frances Shaver had killed herself over Lance, right?"

"Right...."

"And Luke knew all about what happened between her and Lance, right?"

"Right...."

"Then how could he sit around and socialize with the guy?"

"It wasn't like that. They didn't invite Lance to join them. Lance was . . . *Lance*. He'd show up at a dance in his fancy uniform and cruise from table to table, invited or not. If he felt like perching at their table he'd do so, and they'd tolerate his presence. Bob wasn't going to tell him to get lost. Lance was his big brother. Bob idolized him."

Mitch drank some more tea, sorting his way through it. Luke Cahoon had despised Lance Paffin because of what Lance did to Frances. Chase Fairchild had certainly harbored no warm, fuzzy feelings for him—Lance had gotten the future Mrs. Fairchild pregnant. And while Bob was busy looking up to him, Lance was busy scoring with Easy Deezy. And then there was Buzzy. "You said that Buzzy Shaver had to look after his mother after Frances died," he mused aloud. "It sounds as if Lance did a pretty thorough job of messing up the guy's life."

"Buzzy has had more than his share of misfortune," Sheila responded. "His dad, Clarence, died of a heart attack during Buzzy's junior year at Bowdoin. Buzzy had to drop out and

73

come home to run the family newspaper. I had Buzzy as a pupil in two of my English classes. Believe me, he was not a gifted writer. Rather ironic that he ended up being the editor and publisher of a newspaper. Or I always thought so. I mark up a copy of it every week for grammatical errors and typos and I mail it to him."

"I'm sure he appreciates it," Mitch said.

Sheila grinned at him with savage delight. "I'm sure he doesn't."

Bitsy studied Mitch from across the table. "You were about to make a point, weren't you?"

Mitch nodded. "Every man in Bob's circle had a good reason to hate Lance's guts."

"Not just in Bob's circle," Helen pointed out. "Lance damaged a lot of lives. I suppose a few ladies shed a tear after he disappeared. But no one in Dorset, with the exception of Bob, was genuinely sorry to see him gone."

"Except he's not gone," Mitch reminded her.

"No, he's not." Helen was gripping her teacup tightly now. So tightly her knuckles were white. "And we'll be sorry we found him. Sorrier than you can imagine."

"Why is that, Helen?"

"Because he's going to do it all over again, that's why. Lance Paffin will ruin somebody else's life before his remains are put to proper rest in Duck River Cemetery. Maybe more than one life. That man's not done," she warned them, her voice rising with emotion. "I tell you, he's not done!"

CHAPTER 5

SHE MET HIM AT the Kinney Road boat launch, a secluded little spot on the Connecticut River a few miles up Route 156, in the lush farm country north of the village. On warm summer days folks liked to put their kayaks in at the boat launch. On a chilly April day like this one, when there were still chunks of ice floating downriver from northern New England, Des and Mitch had the parking lot to themselves. She leaned against the hood of her cruiser and picked at the Greek salad she'd gotten for lunch. He stood at the river's edge skipping stones with feverish intensity. He was having zero luck but that didn't stop him from trying. Or from thinking he was doing one hell of a job. Mitch was a master of self-delusion when it came to such things. He was, after all, a man.

"Skipping stones is all in the wrist," he explained as he flung one after another into the river. Not a single one of them skipped. They all sank right to the bottom like, well, *stones.* "Happily, my wrists are incredibly strong and flexible, thanks to all of the downward-facing dog I've been doing."

"Yeah, I can see that," Des said, gazing out at the ripple of the current on the water's surface. Except not really. What she was seeing were those skeletal remains in that rotting uniform. That skull with its strands of hair. That Rolex Submariner hanging loose around the bones of the wrist. She shuddered inwardly, certain she would need to draw a picture of it in order to cleanse herself of the memory. But equally certain that what she wanted to draw, *had* to draw, was beyond her grasp. Which totally pissed her off. When Des was pissed off her stomach went into knots, so she set the Greek salad aside and went back to watching the oddly brilliant man in her life fling stones into the river like a crazed speed freak. "Mitch, is it my imagination or are you a teeny bit on the far side of hyper?"

"I am *way* hyper," he responded. "I've been gossiping with the girls for the past two hours. Do you have *any* idea how much sugar I've consumed? Plus Sheila brewed a pot of Earl Gray tea that was *unbelievably* strong. Did you know that *tea* can give you a mondo caffeine buzz? Because I didn't know that *tea* can give you a mondo caffeine buzz. Oh, hey, you want a chocolate chip cookie? Because I have a whole bag of them. Also a bag of Sheila's sour-cherry hermits. They've got walnuts and chocolate chips in them. They're *really* awesome."

"No, thanks. So what did you find out?"

He stopped flinging stones and joined her, parking his generous-sized bum next to hers against the car. "May I say something first?"

"Have I ever been able to stop you?"

"I sure do hate slinking around back alleys this way."

"I would hardly call this a back alley," she said, looking out across the river to the Otter Cove mansions on the opposite bank.

"We're exchanging information on the sly in a remote locale. Honestly? It's as if you're ashamed to be seen with me. I feel used and, well, kind of cheap."

She heaved a slow sigh. "This SIG *is* loaded, remember?"

"Okay, okay. Down to business. Business it is, thin person. For starters, that whole deal this morning with Buzzy Shaver and his Volvo may not have been what you thought. They tell me that he and Beryl Fairchild are quietly keeping company. It's entirely possible that he left his car on Dorset Street so that his nosy neighbors wouldn't hear him driving home at four in the morning. Common practice when you're stepping out, I'm told. I wouldn't know about that. I live on an island. And I don't have any reason to step out." He reached over and squeezed her hand. "May I say how uncommonly green your eyes look right now?"

"May I say it's entirely possible that you'd flunk a drug test right now?" She brought his hand up to her lips and kissed it, showing him her smile. No man had ever made her smile like Mitch did. "Beryl Fairchild is one of the last people who saw Lance Paffin alive that night. I'd love to talk to her. But in order to do that I'd have go through Glynis, who's a lawyer first and foremost. If I want to speak to her mother in connection with an ongoing investigation she'll insist upon being present—in which case Beryl won't give up a thing."

"What, you think she won't be candid in front of her own daughter?"

"What, I know she won't. I'm a daughter. I have a mother. Trust me on this one, big boy."

"Want me to talk to Beryl for you?"

She glanced at him curiously. "Exactly how would you go about that?"

"I'll figure out a way. But hang on because I'm not done talking about Buzzy Shaver."

"There's more?"

"Oh, heck yeah. It seems he had a sweet kid sister named Frances, and Frances and future-Congressman Luke Cahoon were engaged until Lance set his sights on her. Lance convinced her to sail off to Block Island with him for a weekend of illicit humpage. After which he dumped her. She was so shamed and humiliated that she committed suicide."

"So Luke and Lance didn't just go at it over the war in Vietnam."

"Correct. Luke truly hated the guy's guts. He and Buzzy both. And there's more. Lance also got busy with his brother's future wife, Delia, whose nickname around Dorset back in those days was Easy Deezy."

"Okay, this I am loving," Des had to confess. "Do you think less of me?"

"Never. And there's still more. Lance also slept with Beryl. *And* got her pregnant. She had an abortion in Barbados when she was a senior at Wellesley."

Des looked at him in amazement. "Damn, you did good."

"Thank you. I try." He waggled his eyebrows at her, waiting for her to take his cue.

Gravely, she intoned, " 'We all try. You succeed.' "

"Well played. And that's from . . ."

"*Casablanca.* Bogart to Paul Henreid."

"I am so proud of you right now," he said, beaming at her. "Are you going to finish that Greek salad?"

"Help yourself." She looked out at the river again. "So there wasn't one woman in Bob's circle who Lance didn't sleep with."

"There wasn't one woman in *Dorset* who Lance didn't

sleep with—including our very own Helen Weidler, who used to wait tables at the club. He broke Helen's heart. She never let another man get close to her. Trust me, that part's going to depress the hell out of you if you let it." He munched thoughtfully on a forkful of salad. "Lance was a relentless hound. Everyone in town knew it. And yet any number of attractive, perfectly intelligent women fell for him anyway. Speaking as a weight-challenged screening room nerd who registers a 6.5 on the shlub-o-meter I don't understand that. Why would a self-respecting woman sleep with a man who she knows is no good for her?"

A chilly breeze blew in off of the water. Des felt herself shiver inside of her Gore-Tex jacket. "Because we believe we're different from the others," she answered quietly. "And that it'll all work out, even though it hasn't worked out with anyone else before. It's only after we're in too deep that we realize how wrong we've been."

He leaned over and kissed her cheek. "Sorry, I got too close to the bone there, didn't I?"

"That's okay. Brandon is strictly in my rearview mirror now. All I see in front of me is you. And you're not a 6.5 on any shlub-o-meter. You're my idea of a hunk." She shoved her heavy horn-rimmed glasses up her nose and said, "When I spoke with Bob and Delia about the spring dance they mentioned that they'd set Luke up on a blind date that night with his future bride, Noelle. They said Luke had been 'on his own' for a while. But they didn't say a word about Frances Shaver."

"Well, they wouldn't, would they?"

"The reason being? . . ."

79

"They have a scripted version of what happened that night. They've been sticking to that script for forty-seven years. All of them. Every person who was at the table that night. What I'd like to know is who wrote the script." He fell silent for a moment. "Helen's positive that Bob and Chase both knew that Lance was buried under Dorset Street. She overheard them talking on the phone about it years ago."

"So *that's* why she came to see us last night."

Mitch nodded. "And *that's* why Bob always refused to re-grade Dorset Street. He knew. Always has. My guess? They all have. Every person who was there—Bob and Delia, Chase and Beryl, Luke and Noelle. Can you find Noelle?"

"They told me she died. But I'll double-check that."

"One thing we know for sure is that Lance never took the *Monster* out that night. He never disappeared at sea. None of that ever happened. Something else did. And they've stayed quiet about it for all of these years. Chase even went to his grave without saying a word. It's pretty amazing that they've kept this huge a secret for so long. Then again . . ."

Des frowned at him. "Then again? . . ."

"I can think of one good reason why they have," he said. "To protect an even bigger secret."

"What's a bigger secret than Lance's body being buried under Dorset Street?"

"The identity of who killed him. Because *somebody* did, right?"

"We don't know how Lance died. We won't know until the ME tells us. Still, I'm with you. It's pretty incredible. You'd think they would have turned on each other by now."

"Or used it against Luke Cahoon. We have ourselves a

powerful US congressman parked smack-dab in the middle of this, don't forget."

"Trust me, I haven't forgotten."

"Although this may explain why Luke's never taken a run at the Senate. He's had his chances. Chris Dodd and Joe Lieberman have both stepped down in the past few years. Either Senate seat was his for the taking. And yet he's declined to run. Why? Because a Senate run means big money. Special-interest money that comes with special-interest scrutiny attached, as in snarky political operatives combing the man's past for dirt. Luke's congressional seat is safe. No one bothers to mount a serious campaign against him. But if he ran for the Senate then the gloves would come off, and maybe he can't afford that." Mitch polished off the last of the Greek salad. "Will you be talking to him?"

"I doubt that. I'm just the lowly resident trooper who's keeping this investigation warm until the Major Crime Squad can take over."

"And when will that be?"

"Tomorrow, probably."

"That means we can't waste another minute flapping our gums." He hitched up his jeans and started briskly toward to his truck. "We've got to keep on keepin' on. Let's do this thing, Sheriff."

Des smiled at him. "Whatever you say, Deputy Dawg."

Des inhaled the heavy scent of eau de creosote as she bumped her way slowly along the partially graded and rolled surface of Dorset Street that Wilcox Paving had left behind. Outside of the Congregational Church, the gravesite had been tented and the ME's team was hard at work sifting through the soil. Two state troopers remained stationed there to keep people away.

She parked her Crown Vic in front of a wood-framed one-story building a half block from the crime scene. It was painted a creamy yellow with white trim. Two words—THE GAZETTE—were emblazoned above the front windows in an old-fashioned typeface.

Inside, the offices of Dorset's weekly newspaper were stubbornly quaint. The newsroom's walls were lined with vintage oak filing cabinets and framed, yellowing copies of front pages that appeared to date back to the 1920s. Buzzy Shaver's huge, cluttered rolltop desk, which anchored one corner of the newsroom, certainly dated back that far. Some kind of an ancient manual typewriter was parked on it, along with an old, old camera, a pipe rack filled with eight or ten pipes and a tin of Sir Walter Raleigh pipe tobacco. The man's desk was practically a shrine. Hell, the whole newsroom was. Des doubted that the place looked much different than it did back in the old days, with the possible exception of the almost complete absence of people. She saw no sign of Buzzy. The reception desk and four of the five news desks were unoccupied.

The only person in the place was the young, blond-haired guy whom she'd seen trying to take pictures of the skeletal remains that morning. He was perched at a desk on a bright orange fitness ball tapping away at a laptop computer. Three five-by-eight-inch notepads were open before him, their pages covered with scrawled notes. When he noticed her there, he jumped to his feet.

He was tall and broad shouldered. Wore a blue button-down shirt, fleece vest and jeans. "Thanks for coming so soon, Trooper Mitry."

She looked at him blankly. "Excuse me?"

"I just placed the call a minute ago. You *are* responding to my call, aren't you?"

Her cell phone vibrated on her belt now. It was the 911 dispatcher directing her to proceed to the offices of *The Gazette*.

"Actually, I stopped by to have a chat with Mr. Shaver. You are . . ."

"Bart Shaver," he said, extending his hand. Bart had alert blue eyes, a strong jaw and a wisp of a see-through moustache that did him no good whatsoever. "I've been giving Uncle Buzzy a hand around here for the past few weeks."

"So you're Mr. Shaver's nephew?"

"Well, no, not if you want to get technical. He and my dad were first cousins. I've just always called him Uncle Buzzy."

"Okay. How may I help you, Bart?"

"For starters, you can tell me if that was Lance Paffin who was buried out there."

"Where'd you get that idea?"

"I hear things," he said with a shrug.

"They found unidentified remains that may or may not be human. If you have any more questions about that you'll have to call our public information officer. Now what else can I do for you?"

Bart eased himself back down onto the fitness ball, moving his hips gingerly from side to side. "I got thrown from my mountain bike up at Franconia Notch last summer," he explained. "Gorked a couple of vertebrae in my lower back. They still bother me when I sit—unless I sit on this thing. Uncle

Buzzy *hates* the sight of it in his hallowed newsroom. Gives me nothing but grief. Listen, I apologize in advance if it turns out I'm overreacting, but he's sort of disappeared. Hasn't shown up for work today, which is weird considering that newsworthy commotion outside, you know? And he isn't answering his home phone."

Des tipped her big hat back on her head. "How about his cell?"

"He doesn't own one. Doesn't believe in them. I swung by his house about an hour ago and he wasn't there. He also . . ." Bart trailed off, clearing his throat. "He sent me an e-mail early this morning, just before eight o'clock. Which I have to admit surprised me—I wasn't sure he actually knew how to use a computer. He still pecks out his weekly column, 'Buzzy's Buzzings,' on that old typewriter of his. It came from his office e-mail address. So he must have stopped by here before I got in and used one of our desktops. He doesn't have one at home."

"What did his e-mail say?"

"Here, have a look. . . ." He turned his laptop around so she could read what was on the screen:

Don't try to find me, bub. And do me a favor and keep the old Gazoot alive, okay? Love, Uncle Buzzy

She studied the screen, frowning. "The '*Gazoot?*'"

Bart smiled faintly. "That's what I used to call *The Gazette* when I was a little boy."

"Has he been upset about anything in particular?"

"Well, yeah. His health just for starters. He has emphysema from inhaling pipe smoke for all of those years. He's definitely been gloomy about that. And our financial situation sure isn't helping."

"What financial situation is that?"

"*The Gazette* is flat broke. Has been for years. There's no staff anymore in case you haven't noticed—just Uncle Buzzy and me. The only way we've been able to stay afloat this long is because Bob Paffin has been quietly funneling Buzzy money. But now that Bob's no longer first selectman, and doesn't need our editorial support, he's pulled the plug. Kind of cold if you ask me. Those two are lifelong friends. But Bob won't help him out anymore. So we have to fold our print edition at the end of this month, which is a pretty big deal. We haven't announced it to our readers yet, but we'll be converting to an all-online operation. Buzzy hates the idea. He doesn't believe a paper is real unless he can hold it in his two hands. But this has been happening to a lot of community newspapers. We simply can't generate enough ad revenue to support a print edition. I've been helping him make the transition. I really want to keep *The Gazette* going. A community newspaper is vital to a town like Dorset, whether it's on paper or online. How else can we keep the bastards in local government accountable to the voters? The TV stations don't cover town government. The city papers are cutting back on their regional coverage. It's up to papers like ours. And once we go online we can do a much, much better job of keeping up with breaking local news. I can update our home page bim-bam-boom. But, hey, I'm not telling you anything you don't already know. Your boyfriend plays in the big leagues."

"Mitch is a movie critic."

"A movie critic who has a master's degree from the Columbia Journalism School. You know what that makes him, don't you?"

"You mean aside from insufferable?"

"A journalist. It's in his blood, same as it's in mine. I'm one of Mitch Berger's biggest admirers. He writes with verve."

"Yes, he does."

"That's because he's passionate about movies. I feel the same way about Dorset. And I don't know about you but I *love* what our first selectwoman brings to the table. That woman knows her stuff. She also believes in transparency—unlike Bob Paffin. Did you know that he had public works redo his gravel driveway at the town's expense? Real deal. I spent three days over at the town garage poring over their requisition forms and time sheets. He disguised it as a road maintenance project on Frederick Lane. There was no such project. The man ripped us off. I wrote a detailed investigative piece all about it, but Buzzy killed it."

"Did he say why?"

"You mean aside from the fact that Bob's been bankrolling *The Gazette*? He said, 'No one wants to read this crap, bub.' Please don't get me wrong about Buzzy, Trooper Mitry. He's a genuinely great guy once you get to know him, but we have different views about what sort of future we want for Dorset. He wants it to be like it was in the so-called good old days. I want it to become more diverse and inclusive—a living, breathing part of the twenty-first century. I intend to stay put here. As soon as my girlfriend, Mary Ann, finishes up at Vassar we're going to get married and raise our family here. I love this place. And I love that old curmudgeon. My parents have both passed. He's the only family I have. And I'm all he has now that his mom is gone. Me and *The Gazette*. He's not really happy in the Dorset of today. He absolutely detests Glynis, even though he and her mom are close friends. I did call Mrs. Fairchild before I called you. She hasn't heard from him." Bart's brow creased with concern. "I don't mean to put you to any unnecessary trouble but can you please make sure he's okay?"

"Of course. That's my job. Any idea where he might have gone?"

"He does have a fishing shack way out in the woods on the far side of Crescent Moon Pond. Sometimes he goes there when he wants to brood. He built it before the state turned those woods into a nature preserve. It's the only shack out there. Strictly bare bones. No electricity or phone. No road either. The only way to get there is to row your way out."

"Does Mr. Shaver have a rowboat?"

Bart nodded. "Keeps it in his garage. Mounts it on the roof of his Volvo."

"Is he physically capable of rowing himself across Crescent Moon Pond?"

"If he sets his mind to it. Buzzy's a stubborn old coot."

"Have you got a key to his place on Appleby Lane?"

"He keeps a spare in his desk." Bart got up off of his fitness ball and fetched it for her.

"Do I have your permission to enter the premises if he doesn't answer?"

"Absolutely." He looked at her curiously. "You don't suppose this has anything to do with those remains they dug up out there this morning, do you?"

"I don't suppose anything. Supposing isn't my job."

"I'd sure like to see a copy of the incident report from the night Lance Paffin disappeared back in 1967."

"Like I said before, you'll have to call our public information officer."

"Okay, okay. The lid's screwed on tight. I hear you."

"But, listen, I can let you know when the documentation is about to made me public."

Bart brightened. "You mean I'll get it first?"

"You will if you're quick on your feet."

"I'm plenty quick. Hey, thanks."

"No prob." Des started for the door, then stopped. "One last thing, Bart. Does Mr. Shaver own a gun?"

Bart's jaw muscles tightened. "A rifle. He used to go deer hunting a lot."

"Do you know where he keeps it?"

"In his bedroom. It's hanging from a couple of wrought-iron hooks over the closet door. It might be a Remington, but I'm not positive. I don't know much about guns. The truth? I don't like guns."

"The truth? That makes two of us."

Appleby Lane was a mix of the old and the new. There were lovingly maintained farmhouses and center chimney colonials that had been there for more than two hundred years. These were set quite close to the road. There were also more than a few newer trophy mansions set way back behind ChemLawn carpets that were already greening up in weed-free, neon-bright splendor.

Buzzy Shaver's place was one of the old ones, a cramped-looking white farmhouse surrounded by tall cedar trees that really needed to be limbed up. Several of the lower branches were draped right over the roof, shrouding the house in moldy darkness. The house needed a new roof. Its rotting shingles looked like pieces of wet toast. It needed paint and trim work, too. And the fieldstone foundation was crumbling in spots. There was no black Volvo in the driveway. Or in the detached two-car garage, which was open.

Des got out of her Crown Vic and searched the garage. She found no rowboat. Then she started her way toward the front door of the house, feeling the eyes of Buzzy's neighbors on her from behind their curtains. If anyone had anything to tell her they'd mosey on out. But no one did.

She knocked on Buzzy's door and waited. No answer. She used the key that Bart had given her.

It was damp and cold inside. Also incredibly dark for mid-day, what with those tall trees and the heavy curtains over the windows. She flicked on a lamp and found herself in an old lady's house. The parlor was crowded with plush, ornate Victorian furniture. The satin lampshades had tassels hanging from them. Fussy porcelain bric-a-brac was displayed here, there, everywhere. All of it was badly in need of dusting.

Des called out his name. No answer.

She made her way into the dining room, where she found still more uber-Victoriana. An immense glass-fronted sideboard was stacked full of china. Eight matching high-backed chairs were placed around a claw-footed table that was covered with a frayed white-linen tablecloth. The glass bowl that was set in center of the table was filled with wax fruit. Des couldn't remember the last time she'd seen genuine wax fruit.

She called out his name again. No answer.

Although now she could hear a low murmur of voices coming from the back of the house. She made her way through a swinging door into an eat-in kitchen that hadn't been remodeled in at least fifty years. The countertops were tiled in contrasting shades of pink and charcoal. The linoleum pattern on the floor resembled a Spanish omelet. The low voices were coming from a thirteen-inch TV that was tuned to a black-and-white Western on TCM. Sturdy young Tim Holt seemed to be the star. Des realized to her dismay that it had finally happened. She could now walk into a room and instantly identify any old movie's leading man. Clearly, she'd been spending too much time around a certain someone.

The kitchen sink was full of dirty dishes. The faucet drip, drip, dripped. The stovetop looked as if it hadn't been given a proper scrub in six months. She stood there for a moment, hands on her hips, before she flicked off the TV. She tried to silence the dripping faucet, too, but had no luck with that.

Upstairs, she found three small bedrooms and one bath. The first bedroom she came to smelled of face powder and fruity perfume. Buzzy hadn't touched a thing in here since his mother's death, it appeared. It was as if the old lady still lived here. Her perfume, powder and hairbrush remained on her dressing table. Hairs. There were long silver hairs in the brush. The old lady's bed was neatly made. And her clothing was still hanging in her closet. Des pulled open the top dresser drawer and found stacks of carefully folded linen hankies and silk underthings.

Another shrine. The man was into shrines. The only thing missing from this one was Glady Shaver's slippers positioned just so on the floor beside the bed. As Des stood there she found herself shuddering inwardly. It was too quiet in this room. And just a tiny bit creepifying.

Buzzy's bedroom was on the weird side, too. Or at least she found it weird that a grown man still slept in a narrow single bed in the very same room that he'd slept in as a boy. He even had his old, faded Boston Red Sox and Dorset High Fighting Pilgrims pennants hanging above the bed, which was unmade. The room was messy. Dirty clothes were strewn everywhere. And it smelled goaty—the telltale old-man aroma that Mitch so dreaded. A pair of black wrought-iron hooks was mounted over the closet door, just as Bart had said. But no rifle hung there. Des checked under the bed. No rifle. She searched the closet from top to bottom. No rifle. She did find a lady's frilly nightgown and silk bathrobe hanging from a hook on the back of the door, smelling strongly of that same fruity perfume as the room next door. Des didn't ask herself why Mr. Clyde "Buzzy" Shaver had his dead mother's nightgown and robe hanging in his closet. She didn't want to know why.

The third bedroom, which she was guessing had been his sister's room, was now Buzzy's den. Clearly, this was where the old curmudgeon spent most of his waking hours. He kept an oxygen tank in here to help him breathe. It was parked beside a worn leather easy chair set in front of an old twenty-inch Sony TV that was as deep as it was wide. On a shelving unit under the TV was a circa-1995 VCR and a collection of vintage videocassettes. Buzzy seemed to be a big fan of the ribald British TV comic Benny Hill. Also of a British TV sitcom called *Are You Being Served?* Newspapers and magazines were heaped on the floor next to his chair along with a stack of crossword-puzzle books. There were dirty dishes and beer cans on the coffee table.

There was no sign of his rifle.

Des stood there in the damp, silent, creepy house with her hands on her hips. Then she took a deep breath, sighed it out, and decided to rent herself a rowboat.

A stringy old man who worked in the storage shed up at Dunn's Cove Marina was able to help her out. He didn't ask her where she was taking the rowboat. Or why she wanted two life vests instead of one. He was an old Swamp Yankee who didn't ask questions, especially of a black woman in uniform. Just helped her bracket the thing to the roof of her Crown Vic and sent her on her way.

From Dunn's Cove it was less than a mile down Route 156 to the turnoff for Nehantic State Forest. A narrow, rutted dirt road led her to Crescent Moon Pond, which was her idea of a lake more than a pond. It had to be a good half mile across to the densely wooded shore on the other side. Buzzy's shack was not visible from the parking lot. One car sat there in the lot—his black Volvo. It had brackets attached to its roof. No rowboat. The car was unlocked. Keys were in the ignition.

Des was unhooking the rowboat from her cruiser when her cell rang. It was the first selectwoman.

"Des, my mother has just informed me about the visit you paid to Bob and Delia Paffin," Glynis stated forcefully. "I want to assure you that I am 100 percent at your service. There's no way I can be an effective first selectwoman if I don't assist you in any way that I can. I won't stonewall you or circle the wagons simply because my own parents happened to be two of the last people who saw Lance Paffin alive."

"I appreciate that, Glynis."

"*But* I do wish to make two very important points. One, my father was the most decent, ethical man I've ever known. If he knew anything about Lance Paffin's disappearance—and I'm in no way suggesting he did—he would have kept quiet about it not out of complicity, but because attorney-client privilege required him to do so. He would never betray a client's confidence."

"Are you saying that a client of his was involved?"

"I'm saying no such thing. I honestly have no idea."

"Did he ever speak to you about Lance's disappearance?"

"Never. My father was extremely tight-lipped."

"Well, do you think there might be anything in his files that could help us? Notes, journal entries . . ."

"I doubt he would have put anything down on paper."

"Do you mind if we have a look?"

"Not at all—provided you have a judge's written consent."

"That's funny, I could have sworn you just said you wouldn't stonewall me or—what was that other thing, circle the wagons?"

"And I won't. But there are laws about these things."

"What's the other important point you want to make? You said there were two."

"I'd like to be present when you speak with my mother."

"In what capacity?"

"As her attorney."

"Okay, I'll let you know when I'm going to talk to her. Has she ever spoken to you about Lance?"

"Only in a general way. His drowning served as a go-to cautionary tale around our house back when I was a reckless teenager."

"I have trouble imagining you as reckless."

"You didn't know me when I was seventeen." Glynis fell silent for a moment. "Des, may I speak candidly?"

"Please do."

"We're talking about ancient history here. Something that happened long before you and I were even born. Part of me wishes we could just tuck that hideous skeleton into Lance's plot at Duck River Cemetery and forget about it."

"All of me wishes we could do that, Glynis. But we can't. There are laws about these things, too."

Des rang off and muscled the stubby rowboat into the chilly waters of the pond. Thin sheets of ice floated on the surface where there was deep shade. She put one of the life vests on over her Gore-Tex jacket and tossed the other one in the boat, then climbed in and set off, powering the wooden oars through the water. Her muscles welcomed the exercise. It was extremely peaceful out on Crescent Moon Pond on this early spring afternoon. This would have been a pleasant way to spend her time if the circumstances were just a bit different.

When she'd made it halfway out she realized how Crescent Moon Pond got its name. It had a severe crook in its middle. What she'd been looking at from the parking lot was merely the bend, not the farthest bank. As she rounded the bend the other side of the pond came into full view. And so did a small shack. A rowboat was tied up there at a rotting dock. She rowed her way to it and tied up next to it. Got out and started toward the shack, walking carefully on the dock's none-too-sturdy planks. The shack was old, with a rust-streaked tin roof. There was a well with a hand pump out front. Two wooden steps led up to the front door, which was half open. Inside, she found a potbelly stove and a plain wooden worktable that had a couple of wooden chairs placed at it.

Seated at the table with a nearly empty bottle of Old Overholt rye whiskey in his hand was Buzzy Shaver. The old man wore a gray cable-stitched cardigan sweater, white shirt, tan slacks and a glazed expression. A bronchodilator inhaler sat before him on the table. His deer-hunting rifle, a Remington bolt action Model 700 BDL center fire, was positioned on the other chair with its barrel propped on the table and pointing directly at his jowly face. Its walnut stock was pressed against the back of the chair and held in place there by Buzzy's gnarly, muenster-scented bare feet. His two big toes were squeezed around the Remington's trigger. They were trembling.

"I've always wondered if that would work," she said quietly. "I've seen people do it on TV but never in real life."

Buzzy didn't respond to her words for a long moment. Just stared at the muzzle of the rifle. His mind was already somewhere far, far away. He was almost gone. "It'll . . . work," he responded finally, his voice hoarse and slurred. "Stick around and you'll see it for yourself."

"What have you got in there, Mr. Shaver?"

"A thirty-aught-six cartridge." He took a swig from the bottle. "The hell you want?"

"Nothing much. Just came by to say thank you."

"For . . ."

"Leaving me with such a bloody mess. I'm the one who gets to clean up after you, you know. And I'll have to inform Bart."

"My *ball boy*?" Buzzy let out a derisive snort. "My father would turn over in his grave if he saw the stupid orange ball that kid sits on. It's a newsroom, not a day-care center." He let a wheezy sigh, his chest rising and falling, rising and falling. The simple act of breathing was hard work for him. "Or it was a newsroom. The paper is history now. Bart's destroyed it."

"Bart told me he's trying to save it. He loves *The Gazette*. Loves you too, Mr. Shaver. He thinks you're a sweet old guy. But you're not, are you? You're nothing but nasty through and through. If you gave a damn about Bart, or anyone else, you wouldn't blow your face off like this." She paused, her eyes fastened on the old man's trembling toes. "Then again, you did shlep all of the way up here. I guess that counts for something."

"The hell you talking about now?"

"You were alone in your house on Appleby this morning. Had your rifle, a perfectly fine kitchen table, chairs. Why didn't you just do it there? Were you ashamed to take the coward's way out in front of your mother?"

"My mother's dead."

"Really? You wouldn't know it by the look of the place."

"You get out of here," he snarled, flaring at her.

"Happy to, Mr. Shaver. *If* you'll let me have that rifle."

"No!" His shaking toes tightened on the trigger. "Just get out of here and leave me alone. I'm ready to go."

"If you're so ready then what's with the drama?"

He blinked at her, his brow furrowing. "What drama?"

"You had to row all of the way out here, gasping and wheezing. If you're so ready to go why didn't you just chuck your bronchodilator into the pond? You'd probably be dead by now from oxygen deprivation or heart failure. No muss, no fuss. So what is this—a cry for help?"

His gaze returned to the muzzle of the Remington before him. "What have I got to live for? *The Gazette* is gone."

"That's not how Bart sees it."

"Bart's an idiot," he growled. "And I don't think much of his girlfriend either. That is one plain-faced girl. Can't imagine what he sees in her."

"Maybe he loves her."

"I wouldn't know about that."

"You've never been in love?"

"Go away! Just leave me in peace, will you?"

"Afraid I can't oblige you, Mr. Shaver. The State of Connecticut expects certain things of its sworn personnel. One of them is that I'm not allowed to let a cranky, drunk old man blow his face off. Sorry about that." She tipped her hat back on her head, studying him. "You know, I think I've got you figured out. You're trying to serve as a weapon of mass distraction, aren't you? You e-mailed Bart that cryptic suicide note knowing he'd contact me and I'd come looking for you. And that when I found you here, dead, the media would get so caught up in your tragic suicide that they'd forget all about the other thing."

"*What* other thing?"

"The body we found underneath Dorset Street. This is a Hail Mary play. Except you messed up because you're not ready to die. If you were then your blood and brain matter would already be congealing all over that wall behind you. Hell, you had a two-, three-hour head start on me."

Buzzy took a swig of Old Overholt, scowling at her. "I don't know what you're talking about."

"You couldn't do it, Mr. Shaver. Couldn't pull that trigger. It's fine by me. I'm not disrespecting you. But you're sure disrespecting me and mine."

"How so?"

"You don't think we can walk and chew gum at the same time. The media might get distracted, but we won't. We *will* find out what really happened to Lance Paffin on that warm spring night back in 1967."

Buzzy had nothing to say to that. Just stared at the muzzle of the Remington, his toes still trembling on the trigger.

"I understand you and Beryl Fairchild are an item these days."

"Just old friends. She makes me dinner two, three nights a week because I'm no good at cooking. Rents us a movie to watch on TV. Sometimes I fall asleep on her sofa while she's doing the dishes. She doesn't like to wake me because people our age have a lot of trouble falling asleep. So I get home late some nights and I—"

"You park your car on Dorset Street so your neighbors won't gossip."

"This is *Beryl Fairchild* we're talking about, not some barmaid at the Monkey Farm Café. She feels sorry for me," he said morosely. "Always has. I never had much luck with girls. They'd take one look at this face and run for the hills. Mostly, I took care of Mother. Not that I could please the old bitch. Nothing I did was good enough. And, God, the one time I did bring a girl home it was pick-pick-pick the minute Mother laid eyes on her. Pick-pick-pick. Because she was afraid she'd lose me. I was all she had, you know, a-after . . ." He let out a strangled sob. ". . . after Frances died. Frances slit her wrists because of that bastard. Mother was never the same. Life was never the same." He flexed his toes on the trigger, wincing. They'd cramped up on him from the awkward way he was holding them. By now Des was fairly certain she could snatch the Remington away from him. But she didn't want to take that chance. Not if she could avoid it. Especially when he was feeling chatty. "Everyone loved Frances. She believed in people. Believed that all of us are good inside. Lance *wasn't* good inside. He was pure bastard. Had to go after her. Had to have her. It was Luke who she loved. And Luke loved her. They belonged together. But *no* woman one was off-limits as far as Lance was concerned."

"Mr. Shaver, what do you know about his death?"

Buzzy peered up at her, his eyes narrowing. "The same thing everybody else knows. He took the *Monster* out and never came back."

"Were you surprised that we found those remains under Dorset Street?"

"I've been around for a long time. Nothing surprises me anymore."

"And nothing goes on in Dorset that you don't know about. So tell me, what really happened that night?"

He took another swig of Old Overholt. "I have no idea."

"I don't believe you."

"Then don't believe me. I don't care. Because I'll never tell. You can put me in front of grand jury or a goddamned firing squad and I'll never tell. None of us will."

"Who is *us*?"

Buzzy glanced at her sharply before his gaze returned to the muzzle of the Remington. "I'll die before I tell."

"Suit yourself. But not on my watch. I can't let you shoot yourself."

"I've been sitting here like this for over an hour," he confessed. "Can't do it. Can't pull the trigger. You were right a-about . . ." He broke off, coughing. A hacking, painful cough. "I don't have the guts to do it."

"It doesn't take guts to kill yourself. It takes guts to stay alive."

"Wouldn't know about that. I just know I was glad as hell to see you walk through that door. You probably think all of this is pretty funny, don't you?"

"I don't think any of this is funny, Mr. Shaver." With one swift move she reached down and snatched the Remington from its perch on the chair. "Why don't you put your shoes and socks on? We'll row our way back, okay?"

"Are you going to arrest me?" Buzzy asked her defeatedly.

Des shook her head. "I'm going to call the Jewett sisters. They'll come pick you up."

"I'm not going to tell you anything about that night," he warned her. "You can't make me."

"I've got a thermos of hot coffee in my cruiser. We'll have some coffee while we wait for the girls and you don't have to say a thing. Have we got ourselves a deal?"

"Why not?" Buzzy Shaver grumbled in response. "Why the hell not?"

CHAPTER 6

THE DORSET COUNTRY CLUB sat high atop a hill on Mc-
Curdy Road. Considering just how hard it was to become a
member—letters of recommendation from no less than *three*
active members were required—the club really wasn't much
to look at. The golf course was narrow, featureless and decidedly inferior to the course at the decidedly less exclusive Black
Hall River Club in neighboring East Dorset. There were two
tennis courts that no one ever seemed to use. A swimming
pool that was still covered over for the winter. And the circa-
1957 vinyl-sided clubhouse was drably furnished with mis-
matched plaid sofas and worn, threadbare carpeting.

It was a few minutes after two o'clock when Mitch strolled
in with Bitsy, as her guest. The dining room was done serving
lunch. A half-dozen dignified retirees were digesting their meal
in the reading room with their eyes closed and their mouths
open. There was no bar. Instead, the club had a storage cupboard with lockers where members could keep their private
stock under lock and key. The club's thriftier members were
notorious for buying bottom-shelf A&P store-brand Scotch
and transferring the contents to the bottle from a high-end
single-malt.

They found Beryl Fairchild and Delia Paffin alone in the
sunny card room, talking quietly over a hand of gin rummy.

The two ladies acted startled when Mitch and Bitsy walked in, as if they'd just been caught doing something naughty.

Beryl mustered a welcoming smile. "Why, Bitsy, how nice to see you. You're looking well, dear."

"As are you," Bitsy said brightly. "But you *always* do. Some day you'll have to tell me your secret."

Beryl Fairchild was a slender, silver-haired swan of a lady who exuded poise and elegance. Her posture was perfect. Her complexion was smooth. Her features were finely sculpted. She had good, high cheekbones and a wide mouth with a fetching Tierney-esque overbite, as in the actress Gene, not the actor Lawrence. Her eyes were a lovely shade of blue. But they were not the gleaming eyes of a woman who was happily engaged in life's joyous pursuits. They were the eyes of a full-time practicing widow who had seen life and love leave her behind. Beryl was wearing a pale yellow cashmere sweater and tailored gray slacks. A raspberry-colored silk scarf was knotted artfully around her throat to hide whatever age lines were there.

Delia Paffin, aka Easy Deezy, was a hefty, rosy-cheeked woman who, for reasons known only to her, chose to dye her hair the color of Tang. Mitch had encountered the former first selectman's wife several times at cocktail parties and gallery openings. He'd found her to be beady eyed, calculating and nasty. Otherwise he liked her a lot.

"Do you know Mitch Berger?" Bitsy asked Beryl.

"I know *of* you, of course," Beryl said, extending her slim hand to him.

He gave it a gentle squeeze. "Likewise, Mrs. Fairchild."

"Please, make it Beryl."

Delia did not offer him her own boiled ham of a hand. Merely glared at him as if he'd just tracked something nasty onto her pristine white living room carpet.

"I'm giving Mitch our grand tour," Bitsy informed them. "He's thinking about joining."

"There's a considerable waiting list," Delia cautioned him, her voice distinctly chilly.

"Not a problem," he assured her. "I'm a patient man."

"Won't you two sit with us for minute?" Beryl asked.

"Why, thanks, that would be lovely," Bitsy burbled as they sat down at the card table with them. "You know, I've always liked this room the best. It's newer than the rest of the club, Mitch."

"Was it added on?"

"In a manner of speaking," Beryl said. "The original card room burned to the ground back in '92. It was a smaller room and didn't have nearly as many windows looking out at Old Henry's garden. Old Henry was our head groundskeeper here for nearly fifty years. His garden has always been our pride and joy. His boy, Young Henry, still does a wonderful job with it. Not that there's much to see right now."

Mostly what Mitch saw were the thorny stubs of many, many rose bushes set in tidy rows.

"You must come back and see it when it's in full bloom, Mitch," she added. "It's really quite remarkable."

"Did it have to be replanted after the fire?"

"It did indeed." Beryl gazed out at it. "Between the firemen and the workmen it got thoroughly trampled. It's an entirely different garden now."

"How so?"

"Why do you wish to know?" Delia demanded, her jaw clenching.

"I'm interested in gardens." Mitch noticed two gently aged wooden benches artfully positioned amidst the rose bushes. "Those are great benches. Are they teak? I was thinking about buying one. Do they last a long time?"

"*Yes*, they're teak." Now Delia was outright bristling. "Do you always ask so many questions?"

"I'm afraid so. That's how I learn things."

"They last for generations if you take good care of them," Beryl responded politely. "Which Young Henry does. He tucks them away every winter, gives them a good scrub. And in answer to your other question, the garden was enlarged after the fire so as to accommodate more beds. Young Henry is also a good deal less formal than his father was."

"The old garden was much more traditional," Delia allowed. "And properly enclosed, unlike now."

"I see," Mitch said, even though he didn't. Young Henry's garden not only looked plenty formal but was fully enclosed by a neatly manicured waist-high boxwood hedge.

"He's very clever when it comes to making sure something's in bloom all season long," Beryl went on. "Peonies, foxgloves, hollyhocks, what have you. That way there's always sure to be a lovely backdrop for wedding photos. Many, many weddings have taken place in Old Henry's garden over the years. Delia and Bob were married out there."

"By Reverend Marsh," Delia recalled with a nod of her orange head. "On a sunny day in June of 1969. The 14th, thanks to your dear father-in-law."

"Chase's father was club president back in those days," Beryl explained. "When Delia and Bob decided on a date it turned out that another couple had already reserved the garden for their own wedding. Mr. Fairchild persuaded them to choose a different date so as to accommodate Delia and Bob. Chase was Bob's best man, and I was Delia's maid of honor." A wistful smile crossed her lips. "We were married here ourselves a few months later."

Delia's beady eyes narrowed at him. "Bob and I had a visit from your 'friend' this morning. I don't suppose you know anything about that."

"I know everything about it. So does Bitsy." On Delia's look of dismay Mitch added, "But not because of anything the resident trooper told us."

Bitsy nodded. "It's true. We got dragged in all on our own."

Delia let out a sigh. "It's been such a shock. Imagine, Lance *underneath* Dorset Street this whole time."

"How did Bob take the news?" Bitsy asked her.

"Not well. He fainted. Bob's never had a strong constitution, you know. And then he got extremely agitated when an unappetizing young fellow from the medical examiner's office showed up to take . . . what did he call it? A cheek swab? Bob got so upset that I gave him a mild tranquilizer and put him to bed. He's napping now. Or he should be." She glanced at her watch. "I ought to get home to him. I just *had* to get out of the house for a few minutes."

"Of course you did," Beryl said soothingly.

"Bob *idolized* Lance, you see. Lance was his hero. And he died so young that he never had a chance to disillusion Bob."

"Why would he disillusion him?" Mitch asked.

"Because the Lances Paffins of the world always do. Bob only knew him as his vibrant and charismatic big brother. He never had to watch Lance become just another balding, middle-aged fellow with a beer gut who complains day and night about his enlarged prostate. Lance never . . . he never committed the cardinal sin of becoming ordinary," Delia explained, choosing her words carefully.

Mitch wondered if she'd been that careful when she used to shuck her panties in the back seat of Lance's Mustang GT. A giggly pushover, Sheila had called her.

"It occurs to me that I'm being a terrible hostess," Beryl interjected. "May I offer either of you coffee?"

"I'd love a cup," Bitsy said.

"Me, too. But you'd better make mine decaf, please."

"I really should get home to Bob," Delia said.

Beryl said, "Do give him my best. And call me if you need anything."

The two of them exchanged air kisses before Delia left. Beryl went into the small kitchen that adjoined the card room. She returned a moment later with two cups and sat back down, calm and composed. Mitch couldn't imagine her as anything but calm and composed.

He took a sip of his decaf and discovered that it didn't taste even remotely like coffee. He took another sip, frowning suspiciously. "Am I losing my mind or is this *Postum?*"

"Why no," Beryl responded hurriedly. "No, it's not."

He grinned at her. "Yes, it is. And you're a terrible liar. I haven't had a cup of this since my grandmother died. She used to love it." Postum was an instant coffee substitute made from roasted grain. Easier on the stomach supposedly. "But I thought Kraft Foods stopped making it."

"Back in 2008," Beryl confirmed. "Our club manager in those days believed in bulk purchasing. He was very clever that way. Since quite a few of us happened to enjoy it he purchased numerous cartons of it. We still have several tucked safely away. We have to keep them under lock and key or someone will steal them. Unopened jars of Postum fetch quite a sum on eBay, I'm told. Apparently, the Seventh-day Adventists pay top dollar for them. Was your grandmother a Seventh-day Adventist?"

"Sadie Mandelbaum? No, not exactly."

Beryl squinted at him ever so slightly before she turned to Bitsy and said, "Have you lost weight? You're looking thin."

Bitsy let out a laugh. "I'm looking *fat*. Just like my mom."

"Don't speak ill of your mom," Beryl chided her. "She was one of my favorite people."

"I take it you two have known each other a long time," Mitch said.

"Only fifty years or so," Bitsy answered. "Beryl used to babysit me when we both lived on Turkey Neck Road."

Beryl smiled at her. "And you were so naughty. Always testing me. Tell me, how is Redfield doing?"

Bitsy's face fell. "The same."

"Do you have any idea when he'll be released from prison?"

"He will never be released from prison," she stated flatly.

The reason being that Bitsy's husband, Redfield, had kind of conspired to kind of kill someone. His crime, and the ensuing cover-up, had served as Mitch's introduction to life in bucolic Dorset. It was how he and Des met.

Beryl studied Bitsy, tilting her head slightly. "Still, you're doing well."

"Am not. I'm just good at keeping up appearances. I went to the same finishing schools you did, don't forget. And you? How are you and Buzzy doing?"

Beryl let out a gentle laugh. "Do the village hens think we're a hot item? Allow me to assure you that we've never so much as held hands. We're just old friends who happen to get lonesome. And I own a DVD player and Buzzy doesn't. So I fix us dinner and we watch movies from Netflix. He likes old-fashioned British comedies, the broader the better, such as—"

"Wait, wait, don't tell me. . . ." Mitch's wheels began spinning, spinning. "He's a huge fan of the *Carry On* movies, am I right?"

"Why, yes. We watched *Carry on Nurse* just the other night. Buzzy laughed so hard the tears were streaming down his face. That was quite some guess, Mitch."

"I never guess."

"Myself, I prefer something with a bit of romance in it such as—"

"The films of Douglas Sirk?"

Beryl blinked at him in astonishment. "You amaze me."

"And you amaze me."

"Do I? Why is that?"

"Doesn't it bother you that Mr. Shaver hates your daughter?"

"He doesn't 'hate' Glynis."

"He's practically called her a terrorist in *The Gazette*. In fact, I think he *has* called her a terrorist."

"That's just politics, Mitch. It's not personal. Buzzy is a kind, gentle soul. And he gets terribly low now that his mother is gone. He devoted his life to Gladys. He never had a steady girl. Hardly dated at all, in fact. I don't wish to sound cruel but he was never the most attractive thing around. And now he has such appalling teeth."

"He should have taken better care of his gums. Stim-U-Dents, I understand, can be very helpful."

Both ladies were staring at him.

"Sorry, you were saying . . ."

"For all I know he's still a virgin," Beryl confided. "Unless he associated with call girls. Or, you know, went the other way."

Mitch frowned at her. "You think he's gay?"

"If he is, he's never revealed it to a living soul. But, honestly, it wouldn't surprise me one bit."

Mitch took another sip of his Postum. "You were one of the last people to see Lance Paffin alive, weren't you?"

Beryl arched an eyebrow at him. "Why, yes. A group of us were here for the spring dance. They did it up formal in those days. It was always a special night." She hesitated, glancing out the window at Old Henry's garden. "This place has changed very little over the years. And yet it all seems so different."

"Different how?"

"I suppose . . ." She gazed looked down at her long, slim hands. "What I mean is that back then our world seemed so perfect. But there is no such thing as a perfect world, is there? We were merely insulated from life's harsher realities. So young. So privileged. So clueless. We girls were the last of the breed."

"Which breed is that?"

"The ones who were taught to be seen but not heard. We were expected to be decorative, have our babies and keep our opinions to ourselves. We weren't expected to *do* anything. We were the last ones. In fact, it was already changing while I was Wellesley. Several of my classmates were girls of no particular background at all. Sweaty, pimply girls from places like Camden, New Jersey, who studied like crazy and had every intention of attending law school. I was brought up to marry a lawyer, not become one. That's why I'm so proud of Glynis. She's used her mind. And spoken up. All I've ever done is keep quiet. I'm very, very good at keeping quiet." Beryl's blue eyes shimmered at them. "Lance Paffin saw right through me from the moment we met. Somehow, he knew how frustrated and unfulfilled I was. He knew the *real* me better than Chase ever did. Lance was a deeply flawed person. He had this overpowering need to go after other men's women. He was always looking for someone, or something, that he couldn't find. I sometimes wondered if deep down inside . . ." She colored slightly. "If he didn't really care for women at all."

Mitch sat there wondering if this whole business was getting even weirder than he'd imagined possible. "You just suggested that Buzzy Shaver might be gay. Now you're hinting the same about Lance Paffin. You don't think that the two of them were involved, do you?"

"I never think about such things, Mitch. There are a great many things in life that I'd simply rather not know about. All I can tell you is that Lance had his way with any woman he wanted. He had his way with Buzzy's sister, Frances, who was Luke Cahoon's girl." Beryl's face dropped. "When Lance decided he was done with her she fell apart, poor thing. It was terribly sad. And so cruel of him. But that was Lance. If he wanted someone he took her—and to hell with the consequences. He had his way with Delia. She was absolutely crazy about him. And he had *me*, again and again and again. He was . . . extraordinarily well endowed. And very proud of it. And I wanted him so badly that I could barely think about anything else. All he had to do was look at me and I was ready for him. He could have me anytime, anywhere. I didn't care. I just wanted him."

"Would you have married him if he'd asked you to?" Bitsy asked her.

"Never," Beryl answered firmly.

"Why not?" Mitch asked.

"Because Lance wouldn't have been faithful to me. I needed a steady, dependable man like Chase. I'm really quite a disorganized and helpless person. I always have been. Chase looked after me. Now Glynis does. She handles my investments, pays my taxes, makes whatever decisions need to be made about the house and car and so on. I become totally paralyzed if I have to make a decision. I needed a man like Chase, not Lance. We weren't right for each other. We never so much as dated, you know. Never had a meal together or went to a movie. It was strictly about sex. It . . . wasn't that way with Chase," she confessed. "Chase was a dear, sweet man. He was very patient with me, attentive, diligent. Yet I never experienced a single orgasm during our entire marriage. I must have faked ten thousand orgasms."

Mitch sipped his Postum in cautious silence, amazed by Beryl Fairchild's candor. Men didn't talk about much of anything with each other. Women, he was discovering, talked about *everything*. "Did Chase know about you and Lance?"

"If he did, he never let on."

"You two never talked about it?"

"We never talked about it."

"So he didn't know why you made that spring break trip to Barbados?"

Beryl's eyes widened. "How on earth did you . . ."

"Not to worry," Bitsy assured her. "We won't tell Glynis."

"Did Chase know what really happened to Lance that night?"

"If he did he never he never let on," she said again, though with a bit less conviction in her voice this time.

"Do *you* have any idea what happened to him?"

Beryl smiled at him faintly. "The resident trooper instructed you to ask me that, didn't she? She can't ask me about it herself. Not without Glynis watching over me like a pit bull. The answer is no, Mitch. I have no idea what happened to Lance. He told us he was 'stoked' to take the *Monster* out for a sail. And that was the last we saw of him."

"Did he and Luke Cahoon get into a fight that night?"

Beryl pursed her lips. "They argued."

"About the war in Vietnam?"

"About Noelle. Luke never forgave Lance for what he did to Frances. How could he? Luke was on his own for a good long while after she died. Heartbroken, really. Bob and Delia decided to fix him up with Noelle that night. I'd known Noelle for years. She was a lovely girl. Luke liked her right way. Noelle liked him, too. There was a lot about Luke to like. He was a good-looking fellow in a shaggy sort of way. An ex-Marine who was a bright light at Yale Law School. Anyhow, when Lance showed up here Luke was *not* happy to see him. He took Lance outside and told him straight away that that if he tried anything with Noelle he'd kill him. Or at least that's how I heard it from Noelle in the powder room."

"And *did* Lance try anything with Noelle?"

"Well, he disappeared that very same night. So he certainly didn't have a lot of time to work with. Not that Lance ever needed much time." Beryl let out a sigh of regret. "Luke and Noelle seemed so happy together at first. But the marriage just didn't take. Noelle told me she simply couldn't make him happy. The poor man never got over losing Frances. She was the love of his life."

Mitch's cell phone vibrated in his pocket. He looked at it, then excused himself and went over by the windows to take the call.

"I've been trying to get in touch with Beryl Fairchild," Des informed him. "I don't suppose you know where she is, do you?"

"I have a pretty fair idea," he responded, gazing out at the garden. It was too neat and orderly for his taste. Mitch preferred a wild profusion of barely controlled chaos. "Why, what's going on?"

"Buzzy Shaver just tried to reconfigure that icky lower lip of his by blowing his entire head off. I managed to talk him out of it. He's on a twenty-four-hour suicide watch at Middlesex Hospital. I thought she would want to know."

"I'll be sure to tell her. Do you want me to include your use of the word 'icky?' "

"And *then* you and me need to log some serious face time, wild man. If that can be arranged."

"You just talked me into it. Your place or mine?"

CHAPTER 7

"It may interest you to know that Lance Paffin was extremely well hung. Proud of it, too."

Des found herself staring across the table at him in amazement. "How on earth did you . . ."

"Beryl Fairchild just whipped it out, so to speak. She was totally into Lance, by the way. Wanted him more than she's ever wanted any other man—including her husband, Chase. She never experienced an orgasm during their entire marriage."

"She *told* you that?"

"She also told me, and I quote, 'I must have faked ten thousand orgasms.' Which, if I'm not mistaken, was the subtitle of Hedy Lamarr's memoir of her life and times as a Hollywood glamour girl."

They were at her place overlooking Uncas Lake eating big bowls of her lentil soup by candlelight, the better to see the moonlight reflecting off of the lake. On the stereo was a vintage recording of Mary Lou Williams playing live at The Cookery.

"Lance and Luke Cahoon did exchange words out in the parking lot that night," he went on, slurping his soup loudly. "The future congressman warned Lance about making any fast and furious moves on Noelle. Or so Noelle told Beryl."

"Interesting."

"Cool your jets, thin person. There's more. Beryl also hinted that Lance *and* Buzzy Shaver were gay."

"Wouldn't surprise me one bit about Buzzy."

"Why do you say that?"

"Because of what I found hanging from his bedroom closet door."

Mitch gazed at her eagerly. "What did you . . ."

"His mother's nightgown and robe. They smelled strongly of her perfume. There's still a bottle of it in her bedroom, along with all of her clothing. He's never given any of it away. Her hairbrush still has strands of her hair in it."

"Whoa, I'm getting that powerful Norman Bates vibe again. Tell me, did you go down into his basement?"

"Feel free to climb off of the *Psycho* express any time, big boy."

"Beryl thinks that Lance's obsessive womanizing might have been his way of proving to himself that he wasn't gay."

Des nodded. "I knew a guy like that when I started on the job. He hit on every woman he met to convince himself he was straight. He eventually came out. But Lance was a Navy fighter jock. Guys like him didn't come out in those days. Hell, they still don't."

"So it's something to consider." Mitch finished the last of his soup, mopping the bowl with a hunk of bread. "As a possible explanation for what he was doing underneath Dorset Street, I mean. Maybe we've been looking for love and/or hate in all the wrong places." He took a sip of wine. "So listen, I've been hangin' with the girls all day and I've got to ask you something serious. Is there *anything* you don't tell each other?"

"Seriously? No."

"Wow, guys are really boring in comparison."

"Wow, are you just figuring that out?" She pushed up the sleeves of the ancient flannel shirt she had on. It and nothing else. That was what she'd been wearing at her easel when he arrived. She'd scanned several of her crime-scene photos of the skeletal remains and bulldog clipped them to her eighteen-by-twenty-four-inch Strathmore 400 drawing pad. Then made one gesture sketch after another with a graphite stick, using her entire arm, moving nimbly on the balls of her bare feet. She hated every single sketch. There was no freedom, passion, energy, *anything*. She'd gotten so pissed off that she'd practically hurled the damned easel off of her deck into the lake below. "I figured something out tonight. I really, really need to jump my game."

He nodded. "Of course you do. In the immortal words of the late, great Warren Zevon, 'Your shit's fucked up.'"

She peered at him. "You knew that?"

"I know you. I know you've been unhappy with your work for weeks. And you'll stay unhappy until you make a meaningful commitment."

"Meaningful commitment as in . . ."

"Take an extended leave so you can draw full time. Or, hell, quit your job. Because right now you're not giving your drawing the attention it needs."

"I do serve two masters," she acknowledged.

"Three. You're forgetting about me."

She showed him her smile. "Right, how silly of me. You honestly think I should quit my job?"

"I think you're an artist, and that nothing else matters. I

think you should do whatever you need to do. Hell, go to Tahiti for six months if you want. Just know this—whatever you decide, I support you."

"God, you really are the Stepford boyfriend."

"You would never have known that expression if you hadn't met me," he pointed out, beaming at her.

"I also wouldn't have known the meaning of the word *geshrai*. Although I'm still not sure I'm down with all of its nuances."

"Wasn't there a professor at the academy who you really liked?"

"Susan Vail. What about her?"

"Maybe you could study with her one-on-one. While you're trying to decide what to do with the rest of your life, I mean."

"Mitch, do you have *any* idea how much private studies cost?"

"I know how much it'll cost if you piss away your talent. Let's consider it my birthday present to you."

"It's not my birthday."

"Why don't you call her?"

"I'm not sure she'd even be interested."

"Call her and find out."

"I'll think about it."

"Just call her."

She glared across the table at him. Mitch was the kindest man she'd ever known, but when it came to the subject of her artist within he could turn downright fierce. "You can let go of this any time."

"Fine, I'll let go. But I didn't bring it up, remember? You did." He sat back in his chair, gazing out the window at the lake. "You know who I really don't get? Bob Paffin. How could he go on idolizing his big brother when the guy was boinking Delia whenever he felt like it? For that matter, how could Bob marry her knowing that?"

"Very good questions. I don't have any answers. But I do have it on good authority that our former first selectman is a crook."

"Which good authority would that be?"

"Bart Shaver. He's trying to keep *The Gazette* alive as an online newspaper. He thinks that community newspapers are the only way to hold local government accountable to the voters."

"He's right."

"He's a nice young guy. Real dedicated, too. He spent days at the public works garage and nailed Bob cold for using town manpower and resources to regravel his own driveway. But Uncle Buzzy spiked the story."

"And you're telling me this because . . ."

"Bart's pretty much a one-man operation. There's no money to pay staffers. He needs volunteers to help out. And he's a huge admirer of yours. He thinks you write with verve."

"He said that? He actually said *verve*?"

"He did."

"You don't hear that word much anymore," Mitch said grudgingly.

"And you don't meet many people like Bart."

"Well, well. I just may have to look him up."

"I thought you might want to."

"Think you're pretty smart, don't you?"

"Little bit."

"You're not bad looking either—in a leggy, insanely erotic sort of a way."

"It's the shirt," she explained, fingering its frayed collar. "With some women it's silk. With me it's aged flannel. I look good in it."

"You look good out of it, too. I just may have to dive across this table and tear that thing off of you—with my teeth."

She moved her empty soup bowl a judicious eighteen inches over to one side, gazing at him through her eyelashes. "So what's stopping you?"

A brisk tapping on her front door stopped him. Followed by the click of someone unlocking the door. And in walked the deputy superintendent of the Connecticut State Police— the six-foot-four ramrod whose steely gaze could roil the innards of even the most hardened veterans. The Deacon had lived here with her while he was recuperating from coronary bypass surgery and still had his own key. She hadn't figured out a tactful way to ask him for it back. How do you tell your father that you don't want him dropping in on you unannounced because you might be three-fourths naked and just about to have wild sex on your dining room table?

He stood there in her entry hall with a file folder tucked under one arm. Her three live-in cats—Christie Love, Missy Elliot and Kid Rock—sidled over to say hello. Des got up and flicked on a lamp and knew right away that this was no casual social call. There were deep furrows in her father's forehead. His forehead only did that when he was major upset.

She smiled and said, "Evening, Daddy."

"How are you, sir?" Mitch chimed in.

"Feeling pretty good. Please keep eating. Don't let me interrupt your dinner."

"We just finished up. Have you eaten, Daddy?"

"I'm good."

"I didn't ask if you were good. I asked if you've had dinner. There's a gallon of lentil soup in the kitchen. Park it over here and I'll heat it up for you."

He unbuttoned the jacket of his charcoal gray suit—one of six identical gray suits that he owned—and hung it on the coatrack by the door, removing a small notepad from the inside pocket. "Well, if it's not too much trouble."

"No trouble at all," she assured him, first darting into the mudroom for the sweatpants that were hanging in there. Because she was not, repeat not, going to have a conversation with her father wearing a flannel shirt and nothing else. She put the heat on under the soup and sliced some more bread. "How about a glass of wine?"

"None for me, thanks."

She returned with a clean napkin and spoon to find the two men in her life seated there chatting away about the New York Mets' bullpen, or total lack thereof. Mitch got along amazingly well with her rigid and intimidating father. The Deacon liked him, despite the pigment issue, because Mitch was genuine and he was good for her. With Mitch there was no artifice or agenda—unlike Des's ex, Brandon, a lying, scheming slab of ebony out of Yale Law School whom the Deacon had never liked. The man had keen instincts that way.

"I apologize for barging in this way, Desiree," he said as Kid Rock jumped into his lap and curled up there, purring contentedly. He and the big orange tabby were BFFs. "It's about that skeleton you found under Dorset Street."

Her gaze fell on the file folder next to his right elbow. "So it *was* you who Captain Rundle called."

The Deacon nodded. "The man's frightened."

"Of what?"

"Guilt by association. Some cases are widow makers. This one's a career killer."

She narrowed her gaze at him. "Why is that?"

"Because it's a great big steaming pile of dung and there's a US congressman parked right on top of it. And until the Major Crime Squad is able to take it over it's *your* great big steaming pile of dung."

"Sounds like you two need to talk business," Mitch said. "I'll clear out."

"You'll do no such thing," the Deacon said sternly. "Desiree and I understand each other much better when you're around. Besides, I'm guessing you already know ten times more about this case than I do. So please stay put while we conversate."

"Well, okay. Except that's not a real word, sir."

"What isn't?"

"Conversate."

The Deacon stared at him. "Yes, it is. I see it in e-mails all of the time."

"We *converse*. We carry on a *conversation*."

Des cleared her throat. "Mitch . . ."

"Sorry. I'll shut up now."

Des could hear the lentil soup bubbling in the kitchen. She went back in there and ladled out a big bowl of it. Placed the bowl and a full basket of bread before the Deacon and then sat back down.

He sampled the lentil soup and pronounced it excellent before he opened his notepad and said, "I have the ME's preliminary findings. The skeletal remains *are* those of US Navy Lt. Lance Paffin. His mitochondrial DNA sample matches that of his biological brother Bob. The distinguishing injuries that Bob told you of—broken right collarbone and left wrist—were in evidence. And the academy class ring that was around his right ring finger was a class of '62 ring with a ruby birthstone and Lance's name engraved on the inside."

"What sort of condition was his wallet in?" Des asked.

"There was no wallet on him. No ID other than the ring. They're still conducting a search for his dental records, but that's just their way of being thorough. There's zero doubt that the remains are Lance Paffin's."

"Any chance they were able to determine a cause of death?"

"More than a chance." The Deacon flipped through his notes. "The victim sustained a severe premortem skull trauma. His cranial bone was pierced and shattered by a spike-like object."

"A spike-like object," Mitch repeated, frowning at him. "Does that mean somebody drove a nail into the back of his skull?"

"Not exactly. When you're dealing with shattered bone any sort of signature piercing is extremely difficult to come by. But they did find a clean rectangular edge at the entry point, approximately three-eighths of an inch wide. They believe the object was square in shape and tapered, which is to say narrower at its tip than its base. They're estimating it was at least two inches in length. At present they have no idea what such an object might have been."

"Sounds like a square-headed nail to me," Mitch said.

The Deacon peered at him. "A square-headed nail?"

Mitch nodded. "They used to be square in the old days. And tapered. You've been in my cottage. You know those exposed posts and beams of mine? They have a bunch of square-headed nails sticking out of them. I'm guessing the family caretaker hung his tools from them way back when."

"Why on earth would someone drive an antique nail into Lieutenant Paffin's skull?" the Deacon asked him.

"Because they could," Mitch answered with a shrug.

"This is hardly a time for levity, son."

"Who's levitating? The guy left a trail of ruined lives in his wake. To know him was to hate him. And *you* said antique nail, I didn't. They still make square-headed nails. High-end carpenters use them when they're restoring old houses. Although the new ones are made of stainless steel, not iron."

"Daddy, did they find any residue at the entry point? Rust, paint chips? . . ."

"Not a thing. Not after all of these years."

Des puffed out her cheeks. "So Lance Paffin was murdered by a spike-like object. Then someone buried him, took his boat out and wrecked it. No way one person acting alone could do all of that. There had to be at least two of them. Somebody to take the *Monster* out and jump overboard. Somebody else to wait nearby in another boat and fish him out. He couldn't *swim* way back to shore. Not during the month of May. The current at the mouth of the Connecticut River is too wicked."

"It would have taken hours for one man to dig that grave in the middle of Dorset Street by himself," Mitch concurred. "And Missy Lay did say she heard 'men' digging with shovels out there."

The Deacon looked at him in surprise. "There was a witness?"

"Of a sort. Missy was considered to be quite buggy—even by Dorset standards."

"How buggy is that?"

"She drank eight fluid ounces of her own urine every single day and there were suspicions regarding the contents of her Halloween brownies. None of which, to my mind, disqualifies her as a witness."

"Desiree, I think I'll have that glass of wine after all," the Deacon said hoarsely.

She got a glass and filled it for him.

He took a small sip. "Here is the reality of our present situation: I am deputy superintendent of the Connecticut State Police. And you, Desiree, are the resident trooper of this place. *We* are this investigation. How we conduct it will reflect on the character of the institution that it has been our honor to serve."

She studied him carefully. "Where are you going with this?"

The Deacon glanced down at the file folder on the table. "In my review of Lieutenant Paffin's case file from 1967 I discovered an appalling lack of professionalism. The responding troopers spoke to two employees of the country club who informed them that not only were Lieutenant Paffin and a group of his friends drinking heavily that evening, but that a quarrel took place out in the parking lot. Yet not one of his friends was questioned about this quarrel after the lieutenant was reported missing. Not one of them was questioned *at all*. There was no follow-up. There are no witness statements. No re-interviews with the club's staff. They didn't canvass the neighbors of the Dorset Yacht Club to determine if anyone heard or saw anything that night. They didn't examine the trunk or the seats of the lieutenant's Mustang for blood or other trace evidence. This whole damned file reeks of winky-wink."

Mitch shook his head. "What's winky-wink?"

"Exactly what it sounds like, Mitch. A crowd of wealthy young blue bloods getting preferential treatment instead of the tough, hard, investigative scrutiny that was clearly warranted. I've even found indications of an outright cover-up."

"What indications, Daddy?"

"After the wreckage of the lieutenant's sailboat was found our crime-scene technicians were sent to the site to gather trace evidence. The boat's tiller was dusted for fingerprints. It was made of laminated ash. Would have yielded good prints. Or should have. Yet, somehow, the fingerprints were misplaced. And our lead investigator, a Sgt. Dave Stank, quit the state police three years later to become chief of staff for a newly elected US congressman named Pennington Lucas Cahoon. Stank remained Cahoon's chief of staff until he left in 1989 to take a higher-paying job as a lobbyist for a defense contractor."

"Is Stank still alive?" Des asked.

"Passed away in 2007." The Deacon sat there in heavy silence for a moment. "Obviously, this reflects poorly on how the Connecticut State Police went about its business in those days. And now, well, we have a situation. We've uncovered the murdered remains of a US Navy lieutenant who disappeared after a night of heavy drinking with friends. And one of those friends just happens to be a powerful US congressman. Once we go public with the ME's findings this will get hot in a hurry. I am talking front-page news. We'll have the FBI crawling all over it. Probably NCIS as well. We have a very narrow window of opportunity to get this right. I'm going to slow walk the ME's findings over to the Major Crime Squad tomorrow. That'll buy us a few precious hours of time," he said, gazing across the table at her. "And give you a chance to have a friendly, informal chat with Congressman Cahoon. I've just conversated . . . I'm sorry, *conversed* with his chief of staff. The congressman will be making an appearance at the senior center in Fairburn in the morning. His schedule is in this folder along with the case file. You have permission to speak with him about the remains that you've found under Dorset Street. I made no mention of the ME's findings. As far as the congressman knows we're still completely in the dark. If he knew how much we know he'd lawyer up and we'd get nothing out of him."

"This sounds kind of devious," Mitch said.

"Only because it is," the Deacon responded, grimacing. "You've met him before, am I right?"

Des nodded. "He was grand marshal of our Memorial Day parade last year."

"And you're a small-town resident trooper who doesn't realize what she's stumbled her way into. Be polite. Be respectful. And be very, very careful. We have to assume that

Congressman Cahoon knows what really happened that night. He may even have been an active participant. I won't be able to keep this under wraps for long, Desiree. We have, at most, twenty-four hours before the curtains are thrown open and the sunlight starts shining on this . . . this . . ."

"Great big steaming pile of dung?" Mitch offered helpfully.

"Exactly."

"Forgive me for saying this, sir, but I'd think you would be eager to expose that this sort of winky-wink rich people's justice used to go on. Still does, for all I know."

The Deacon glared at him. "Because I'm a person of color, you mean?"

"Well, yes."

"I'm deputy superintendent of the entire state police, Mitch. That makes me color-blind. I cannot allow myself to have a racial agenda."

Des studied her father guardedly. "Exactly what is it you want me to do?"

"Make this case go away before it gets kicked to the Major Crime Squad. You have until the end of tomorrow."

"I won't be part of any cover-up."

"Don't you think I know that? That's why I've come to you. You're the one person who I can trust. Put this to bed, Desiree. Do it by the book. But do it on the down low—if you can."

"And if the down low isn't an option?"

"Then scream your head off. Just be mindful of the reputations of the men and women who've come before us and who will serve after we're gone. The credibility of our entire organization—past, present and future—is at stake here."

"Oh, is that all?" On his stony silence she said, "Daddy, please tell me that you feel a tiny bit weird about this."

His jaw muscles clenched. "If this job was simple and easy then—"

"We wouldn't be getting paid good money to do it. *We'd* be the ones paying *them*." She'd only heard him say those words about ten thousand times.

"Desiree, if you can figure out what in the hell happened that night you will make everybody happy."

"Even you?"

"Especially me. Do we understand each other?"

She sat there in grim silence, her stomach in knots.

"I didn't hear an answer, young lady."

"We understand each other."

CHAPTER 8

MITCH TOTALLY LOVED THE whole idea of Dorset Street being a dirt road again. It was as if the historic district, with its antique homes and quaint old commercial establishments, had been zapped a hundred years back in time, when horse-drawn carriages clip-clopped their way along the village's main thoroughfare and life was a whole lot simpler and slower. He bounced his way gleefully past Town Hall in his Studey pickup, savoring that he couldn't drive faster than fifteen mph without doing serious harm to his various and sundry spinal vertebrae. Apparently, he was the only one in town who felt this way. The other drivers who he encountered on this bright blue, frosty morning looked supremely annoyed by the appalling inconvenience. But they were *grown-ups* who were too preoccupied and hassled to notice how much fun they were having.

He felt sorry for them.

He'd driven past *The Gazette* a million times but had never gone inside. As he walked through the door now, Mitch immediately sensed the uptick in his pulse that he always felt whenever he entered a newsroom. For him, there was something magical about a place where the news was gathered, written and disseminated to the public. Didn't matter whether it was a big city newsroom or a small town one. And *The Gazette* was definitely small town. It reminded him a lot of the boondocks newspaper that Kirk Douglas got himself banished to in *Ace in the Hole*, one of Billy Wilder's best films. Certainly his nastiest. There were old oak desks. Rows of oak filing cabinets lining the walls. Glass-fronted bookcases filled with bound volumes of back issues. A painted tin sign hanging from the wall that read NO WHISTLING ALLOWED, which was an old newsroom superstition that harkened back to the days of Horace Greeley. Another painted tin sign—CURSING PERMITTED—was apparently Buzzy Shaver's idea of humor. Buzzy's immense rolltop desk anchored one corner of the newsroom. A black Underwood manual typewriter was parked atop it. So was a circa-1940 Graflex Speed Graphic camera with a flexible bellows and a flash attachment that was the size of a dinner plate. There was an actual paste pot on the desk with a brush embedded in its lid. A coffee mug filled with red grease pencils. Mitch was willing to bet that the old editor still kept a supply of yellow copy paper tucked in a drawer somewhere. Also carbon paper. Assuming somebody out there actually still made carbon paper. Next to the desk stood a hat rack with a couple of battered old fedoras hanging from it.

It was eerily silent in the newsroom. No reporters were seated at the desks. No phones were ringing. The only person in the whole place was a young guy with blond hair who was perched on an orange fitness ball pecking away at a laptop. He stood up when he noticed Mitch there. He was tall and athletically built. Good looking. No doubt always had been.

He smiled with his whole jaw in that practiced, phony way male models do. Mitch hated him on sight.

"This is a real honor, Mr. Berger. I'm Bart Shaver, sir."

"Call me Mitch. And cut out the 'sir' stuff. You're making me feel like I'm forty or something."

"Sure thing, sorry." He treated Mitch to his big-jawed smile again. "I'm just kind of in awe."

"You can cut that out, too. I'm the one who's in awe. This place is incredible. I'll bet you still have a darkroom, right?"

"Back through there." Bart gestured to a doorway with his thumb. "Not that we use it anymore. Everything's digital now. The printing press used to be back there, too. They printed every edition of *The Gazette* right here on the premises in the old days. Sometimes when the weather's damp I swear I can still smell the ink. But that era is long gone," he said regretfully. "And we're folding what's left of our print edition, as you may have heard. Can't afford it anymore. Uncle Buzzy's incredibly bummed."

"I understand that he had to be hospitalized."

Bart nodded. "But he's doing much better today. They're releasing him this morning. I sure am grateful to the resident trooper for coming to his rescue. I guess he just got overwhelmed by the reality of what's happening—even though I'm doing everything I can to make the transition as smooth as possible." He glanced around at the empty newsroom. "Uncle Buzzy used to employ two full-time reporters, a photographer, a managing editor and an advertising manager. Now there's just me, and I haven't drawn a salary since back on the 11th of never. But I'm convinced that we can keep *The Gazette* viable as an online paper. If I didn't believe that I wouldn't be here. And I want to be here. I love this paper. Where would Dorset be without us? Who would record the births and deaths? Where would you get your school bus schedules and your latest Kiwanis Club news?" Bart Shaver was such a true believer that Mitch was warming to him in spite of himself. "*The Gazette* is a vital part of this community. Always has been, always will be. We're going to be fine."

"Even though you have to put it together all by yourself?"

"That's not entirely true. A couple of Uncle Buzzy's fishing buddies help out a bit when they're awake and sober. One of them has been talking to our local advertisers, the other keeps tabs on society news. Or tries. It's the ladies who really know what's going on, but for some reason I can't get any of them to help me. Except for Mrs. Grossel, the faculty advisor for the high school paper. She's recruited her students to handle our sports coverage and youth news. I have help, Mitch. Really, I do." He trailed off, running a hand through his floppy hair. "It's just not the kind of help that I need."

"What kind is that, Bart?"

"I grind out a ton of articles every week. I sure could use someone to give them the once over. Our masthead says that Uncle Buzzy's the editor of *The Gazette*. But what with his health and all he's really not up to it anymore." Bart gave Mitch a sidelong glance. "You went to Columbia J-school, didn't you?"

"Well, yeah."

"So you know everything there is to know about editing other people's copy."

"I know a bit," Mitch acknowledged. "But my plate's kind

of full right now. I'm writing a lot of articles myself every week. Plus I've got my Web site, Facebook page, Twitter account and a book under contract."

"I understand. You're hot stuff."

"That's not what I meant, Bart. I'd like to help you out. I'm just incredibly busy."

"Sure, whatever," Bart said with a shrug of his broad shoulders. "So what are you doing here?"

"I wanted to talk to you about wedding photos."

"Don't tell me you and the resident trooper are getting—"

"Okay, I won't. Because we're not. But when local couples do get married you typically run a wedding photo, don't you?"

"Absolutely. That's our bread and butter."

"Do you archive those photos?"

"Uncle Buzzy's a pack rat. Never throws anything away."

"Even a wedding photo from the 1960s?"

Bart eyed Mitch curiously. "Whose wedding photo are you looking for?"

"A couple that was married in Old Henry's garden at the country club in June of '69. The 14th, to be exact."

"A couple named . . ."

"Bob and Delia Paffin."

Bart let out a hoot. "I am *so* glad the voters finally booted that fossil out of office. He was a do-nothing *and* a crook. I nailed him cold for misappropriating town resources to re-gravel his driveway."

"I heard about that."

"Uncle Buzzy wouldn't print it."

"I heard about that, too."

"Why do you want to see the Paffins' wedding photo?"

"I had a notion about something."

"And you're not going to tell me what that notion is, are you? That's cool. I'm happy to help a colleague—assuming you give me the story first."

"Who says there's a story?"

"I say there's a story. Something's going on or you wouldn't be here looking for a photo from the Paleozoic era." Bart went to one of the glass-fronted bookcases and removed a bound volume of back issues from June of 1969. He laid it open on an empty desk and leafed through it until he arrived at the weddings for the week of the 14th. "By God, Bob was a geeky-looking doof, wasn't he?" He spun the bound volume around so Mitch could get a good look at Bob and Delia Paffin posed together in Old Henry's garden on their wedding day.

"Indeed. I'm amazed he could find a shirt collar big enough to fit over that Adam's apple."

The proud, squinty young groom had his arm around his zoftig new bride, who was twice as wide as Bob even way back then. Her eyes gleamed at the camera in monumental triumph.

The paragraph of copy beneath the photo was standard society-page stuff. The bride, Miss Delia Ann Blackwell, daughter of Stephen and Laurel Blackwell of Dorset, had been attended by her maid of honor, Miss Beryl Beckwith. The happy couple planned to honeymoon on Sanibel Island, Florida, before taking up residence in Dorset where the groom, whose best man had been Mr. Chase Fairchild, was an associate of Paffin Realty.

Mitch studied the photo of the happy couple, which had been cropped tight at their shoulders and waists. Too tight.

"Bart, do you suppose there were other photos of them taken that day?"

"Sure. Probably an entire roll."

"Do you think Buzzy kept them?"

"Photos and negatives are stored in those filing cabinets over in the corner. Knock yourself out. I have to get back to work."

Mitch poked around in the oak cabinets for a while before he located the file that contained all of the black-and-white wedding photographs the newspaper's photographer had snapped in June of 1969. There were quite a few weddings that month. Bob and Delia's was the only one high-toned enough to be held in Old Henry's garden. And he found the eight-by-ten glossy print of the photo that *The Gazette* had run, crop marked with a red grease pencil. What had been cropped out were the opulently blooming rose bushes that the couple had posed in front of. He also found two other eight-by-ten glossies that hadn't been used. These were less formal shots of the newlyweds and a few close friends grouped around those teak garden benches that were still there. Some of the friends were standing. Some of them were seated. All of them were sipping champagne. Mitch recognized Buzzy Shaver and his liverish, low-hanging bottom lip instantly. The old editor had worn a cowlicky crew cut back in those days that was reminiscent of the young Jerry Lewis. Mitch also recognized the maid of honor, Beryl Beckwith, who was as gorgeous as he'd been led to believe. A total knockout. The young guy holding hands with her had to be Chase Fairchild. Glynis was a dead ringer for him. Chase had been fair-haired and on the short side, barely as tall as Beryl. But good looking in an earnest, all-American sort of way. Luke Cahoon was there, too, sporting a mane of hair that fell to his shoulders. The future US congressman looked like a wild-eyed hippie beside his scrubbed country club friends. The willowy, dark-haired beauty standing with him was likely Noelle, the woman he married.

Mitch studied them one and all, these people who Beryl Fairchild had characterized as young and privileged and insulated from, what was it, life's harsher realities. *Back then our world seemed so perfect.* Mitch studied the garden, too, which was for damned sure plenty perfect. Snipped and manicured, not a leaf or petal out of place. A traditional garden, Delia Peck had called it. Properly enclosed.

Bart sidled over toward Mitch, his reporter's curiosity getting the best of him. "Find what you were looking for?"

"Don't know. Have you got a magnifying glass?"

Bart pulled one from the top drawer of his desk and handed it to him. Mitch held it over the photos, studying each of them closely.

"Uncle Buzzy hasn't changed much, has he?" Bart said. "It's a shame he never got married. He sure seems lonely."

"Sure seems . . . hunh?" Mitch murmured distractedly, his wheels spinning as he moved the magnifying glass this way and that.

"But you're not interested in him, are you? What *are* you . . ."

"Old Henry's garden." Mitch tapped the photo with his finger. "It doesn't look like this anymore. Got completely replanted after they had a fire in '92."

Bart frowned at him. "And this is significant because . . ."

"These days it's enclosed by a boxwood hedge. But back in '69 it was 'properly' enclosed."

"What's that supposed to mean?"

"It was surrounded by a low wrought-iron fence, see? Looks to me like it was two feet high. Maybe two and half." Mitch offered him the magnifying glass. "Take a look for yourself."

Bart took the glass and peered closely at the fence. "Okay, I'm looking at a wrought-iron fence. So what?"

"It's a *spiked* wrought iron fence, that's so what. Do you mind if I hold on to this photograph?"

"Not if you promise to tell me what you're up to. I don't get it, Mitch. Why do you care so much about that fence?"

"Because it's not there anymore. Is there any way to find out what happened to it?"

Bart tilted his head at him quizzically. "Does this have something to do with Lance Paffin's body being found under Dorset Street?"

"That information hasn't been made public yet."

"True enough. But I hear things. And you didn't answer my question."

"You didn't answer mine either."

"This is Dorset, my friend. Nothing ever gets tossed. That fence probably found a home somewhere else in town. Young Henry might know where. Do you belong to the club?"

"Not a chance. Why, do you?"

"Buzzy does. So they let me have the run of the place. Want me to talk to Young Henry for you?"

"I can't ask you to do that."

"You didn't ask. I'm volunteering. Maybe some day you'll

do me a favor in return. Like, say, read a few stories for me. Deal?"

"Deal." Mitch handed Bart his business card. "My landline and cell numbers."

"I'll be in touch." Bart flashed his big-jawed smile at Mitch. "Know what? Something tells me I'm going to be seeing a lot more of you."

Mitch stood there in the middle of the old-time newsroom, soaking up the magical elixir of its atmosphere. "Know what? Something tells me you may be right."

CHAPTER 9

THE SENIOR CENTER IN Fairburn was a beautiful new facility—which meant that Des was there ten whole minutes before she wanted to sprint out into the road and hurl herself in front of the nearest oncoming car. She had a bit of a thing when it came to senior centers. She respected older people. And respected the services that were provided at the centers, mostly by neighborly volunteers. Yet the places gave her the jimjams. Partly it was the hushed stillness. Older people don't move around a lot or make much noise. Partly, it was the suffocating air. There's no such thing as an open window at a senior center. But mostly it was just an overwhelming sense of dread that one day soon she, too, would find herself caged in just such a temporary holding center for the soon-to-be departed.

All she could think about was fleeing.

It had taken her forty minutes to drive to Fairburn, an old brass mill town that was about twenty miles inland from Mystic Seaport. Eastern Connecticut was comprised of two completely different worlds. There were the coastline towns such as Dorset. Lovely, prosperous places that were popular summer destinations. And then there were the landlocked towns to the north such as Fairburn, which had once been thriving mill towns and were now just a tattered assortment of economically depressed backwaters with few job opportunities. If young people wanted to make a life for themselves they had to move elsewhere.

But Fairburn's new senior center was state of the art, thanks to the strenuous efforts of US Congressman Luke Cahoon, whose district encompassed not only the shoreline towns but also Fairburn and a dozen other struggling towns just like it. There was a fully equipped nurse's station. A recreation room with a giant flat-screen TV. And a cafeteria where hot breakfasts and lunches were served up daily by a crew of volunteers.

Today, one of those volunteers serving up scrambled eggs, sausage links and oatmeal was the seventy-three-year-old congressman himself. It was a made-for-the-media event. The local TV news crews were all set up and ready to capture Congressman Cahoon as he ladled out oatmeal and bromides about the future of Medicare. The congressman was scheduled to spend no more than thirty minutes at the center assuring his older constituents that he was in DC fighting for their interests. Then he'd be whisked off to Electric Boat in Groton to assure the workers there that he was in DC fighting for their interests.

"I am so happy to see so many smiling young faces here this morning," the congressman exclaimed as the news cameras rolled.

The four dozen or so old-timers who were gathered there—most of them ladies—squealed with delight.

"And I'd like for all of you to know that I am always—"

"Hang on a sec, Congressman!" a reporter from Channel 8

bellowed. "We didn't have sound. You'll have to start over again."

Luke Cahoon didn't so much as blink. He was a consummate pro whose job was playing a role for the cameras. If he was told to say his lines again then he said them again—calmly, graciously and convincingly. When viewers saw this little snippet on tonight's news they'd have no idea that what they were watching was a retake of a staged event.

Washington, as Mitch was fond of saying, was nothing more than Hollywood for the homely.

Luke Cahoon was tall and lanky with shaggy eyebrows, a long blade of a nose and a lopsided smile. He combed his silver hair across his forehead in a style that harkened back to Bobby Kennedy. He was dressed in a rumpled gray flannel suit, white button-down shirt and striped tie. Wore a pair of reading glasses on a chain around his neck, and the relaxed air of a man who'd become a pillar of his generation. Back in 2000 his name had even been floated as a potential running mate for George W. Bush. The congressman had vast foreign-policy experience and decades of service on the Armed Services Committee. He was a courtly, affable moderate who got along well with members of both sides of the aisle. But Bush veered hard right and chose Dick Cheney instead.

And so today Luke Cahoon was in Fairburn ladling up oatmeal and schmoozing with the oldies. "What can I get for you this morning, young lady?" he asked the white-haired lady who stood before him with her tray, dazzled by his star presence. "And how about *you*, dear?" he asked the next lady in line, smiling, smiling. Give it up for him—the man knew how to work a room. When he spotted Des standing there he never stopped smiling. "Master Sergeant Mitry, I'll see you outside in five minutes." And then kept right on working it. "Say, that is some kind of a lovely sweater you're wearing, dear. Knit that yourself?"

The news vans were all clustered together in the parking lot, which overlooked a soccer field that was attached to the community center next door. The congressman's humongous black Chevy Suburban was parked just outside of the door for a quick getaway. His driver/bodyguard, a bulky man in his fifties, sat behind the wheel waiting for him. A retired cop by the look of him. A state police cruiser on escort detail idled there next to the Suburban. Des didn't know the young trooper, who was out of Troop E in Montville. But she did know that the Deacon would scorch his ears off if he caught him reading a magazine like he was.

The congressman was punctual. Precisely five minutes later he came striding out of the senior center trailed by two young aides. One was a ferret-faced guy with an officious air about him. The other was a clenched-looking woman who was barking into her cell phone. His driver got out and opened the back door of the Suburban for him.

"Tom, why don't you go inside and grab yourself some chow?" the congressman suggested. "Steve, Polly? I'm going to need the car for a few minutes, okay?" On their surprised looks he said, "Get in, Master Sergeant Mitry." She got in. He joined her in the roomy back seat and closed the door, gazing at her admiringly. "You wear that uniform well. Is it custom tailored?"

"No, sir."

"Yet you seem at home in it, unlike most of the female troopers who I've encountered. West Point, weren't you?"

"Yes, sir."

"Perhaps that explains it. I want you to know that I truly appreciate the job you've been doing as Dorset's resident trooper. You approach your work with the same mind-set that I have. You're a uniter, not divider. And I like your style. Bob and Buzzy do not. In fact, they never miss an opportunity to tell me just how much they detest you. I think you scare the crap out of them, if you don't mind me saying so."

"I don't mind at all."

He flashed a smile at her. "I also want to thank you for keeping an eye on the family homestead on Johnny Cake. I treasure that old house."

"It's a lovely home. Or it sure looks that way from the outside."

"You haven't been inside? Hell, you'll have to come to tea one of these days. Noelle and I restored it from top to bottom after we were married. Our daughter, Katie, spent the first two years of her life there, not that she remembers."

"Does it have exposed chestnut beams like so many of the old places do?"

He nodded his head. "In the taproom."

"I'll bet those beams are full of those old square-headed nails. My friend Mitch's place is."

Luke Cahoon narrowed his gaze ever so slightly. "Why are we sitting here in Fairburn talking about square-headed nails?"

"No particular reason, sir. I just find them charming."

He glanced out the window at the soccer field, which

hadn't greened up yet. The grass still looked pale and dead. A layer of high, thin clouds had started to move in, dimming the morning sunlight. "Those *are* Lance Paffin's remains that they dug up, correct?"

"Correct. The DNA results leave no doubt. We're continuing to keep his identity under wraps until the ME can finish going about his business."

"Has he been able to determine what happened to Lance?"

"I haven't seen his preliminary finds yet," Des answered truthfully.

"Well, what in God's name was Lance *doing* under there?"

"Not a whole heck of a lot."

The congressman glared down his long nose at her. "Sarcasm? You show up here requesting face time with me so you can pitch sarcasm? Lance Paffin was a *friend* of mine."

"Really? That's not how I've heard it."

Calmly, he laced his fingers together around his bent left knee. His socks sagged. Des could see three inches of pale, hairless shin above them. "Exactly what have you heard?"

"That you and Lance had an argument the night he disappeared."

Luke Cahoon shrugged his shoulders. "We always argued. The man was a total ass when it came to certain subjects."

"Certain subjects such as Noelle?"

"We argued about all sorts of things."

"Such as Noelle?"

"*Yes*, Noelle," he acknowledged impatiently. "That was the night Noelle and I met. She was a school chum of Beryl's. I liked her right away. She was the first girl I'd liked ever since

I'd . . ." He broke off, his face darkening. "I told that preening peacock of a flyboy to stay away from Noelle or I'd kill him with my bare hands. I meant it, too. I've committed murder, Master Sergeant. I killed at least eight enemy soldiers in combat—that I know of. But Lance Paffin was the only man who I've actually said those words to in my entire life."

"Because of what he'd done to Frances Shaver?"

"You're damned right."

"Did you and Lance come to blows that night?"

"Not a chance. Lance didn't care enough about any woman to put up a fight for her. Plus he was a coward at heart. Any man who could behave the way he did toward Frances is a coward. There was no fistfight. Just an exchange of words out in the parking lot."

"And then what happened?"

"He laughed me off and went trolling for other prey."

"Anyone in particular?"

"Not that I recall."

"Congressman, what really happened to Lance Paffin that night?"

"I have no idea. All I remember is that he was 'stoked' to take the *Monster* out. It was quite late and we'd all had a lot to drink. No one else wanted to go with him."

"Not even his brother Bob?"

"Bob doesn't go out on boats. He gets seasick."

"And then what happened?"

"Lance took her out by himself and was never seen again. End of story."

"So you have no idea how his body came to be buried underneath Dorset Street?"

"Master Sergeant, you asked me what I know. I just told you. Let's move this along, shall we?"

"Sir, we've reviewed our case file from 1967 and found some red flags. The Lance Paffin investigation was not handled in a way that the state police can be proud of."

He drew back from her, studying her curiously. "So that's why you're here. You're doing your father's bidding, aren't you? He's trying to bypass the Major Crime Squad and keep it quiet. Of course he is. He's an organization man. That's what organization men do."

Des kept her face a blank. "I'm simply here to ask you the questions that you're going to be asked again approximately twelve hours from now—in much less private surroundings."

"Questions such as . . ."

"Fingerprint evidence taken from the tiller of the *Monster* somehow managed to disappear. And the lead investigator, Dave Stank, somehow managed to reappear as your chief of staff when you were elected to Congress."

"You're thinking that it doesn't look very good."

"I'm not the only one who'll be thinking it."

"I can assure you there was no quid pro quo," he said mildly. "The Stankinator was a good man. Smart, energetic and focused. He made a strong impression on me during that investigation."

"*What* investigation, Congressman? There was zero follow-through."

He let out a pained sigh. "After I was voted in, Dave reached out to me and mentioned that he was looking for a new career opportunity. I gave him one. Any subsequent success that he enjoyed was due entirely to his own hard work. Beyond that, I wouldn't care to comment further."

"That's your privilege, sir. But you *will* be asked these questions again later today. And once you get the Major Crime Squad, you get the media. There will be scrutiny. A lot of it. And it won't be pretty."

"And I couldn't care less," he said. "Before you waste any more of our time, Master Sergeant, I'm going to tell you something that no other human being on this planet knows. Not even those three incredibly loyal people who I just kicked out of this vehicle. I am formally announcing my retirement from the US Congress at 5 PM today, effective immediately. Absolutely no one else knows about this. If word leaks out before I have a chance to make my announcement I'll know who the source was and I'll have your badge. Do you understand?"

"Not exactly. Is this because of the Lance Paffin matter?"

"Officially, I'm retiring because I want to spend more time with my family. Not very original, I'll grant you, but it'll have to do. My daughter, Katie, and her husband Ken live up in Burlington, Vermont, with my three grandkids. I'm a complete stranger to those kids. I'd like for them to get to know me. I'd like to write my memoirs. Maybe teach a class on modern governance at Yale if they'll have me."

"And how about unofficially?"

"Let's just say I'm getting out because I can't bear to go through this again."

"Go through what, sir?"

"I fought two tours of duty in 'Nam, Master Sergeant. I

saw things that no human being should ever have to see. Yet nothing that happened to me over there compared to the pain I felt when Frances took her own life. I'd loved her with my heart and soul ever since I was a boy. What Lance did to her . . . that was the single worst thing I've ever experienced. I can't go through it all over again. I can't let the media drag her name through the mud simply because of my own high profile as a US congressman. I won't let Frances be used that way. She was the only woman I've ever loved. There was never anyone else."

"What about Noelle?"

"I was *smitten* by Noelle," he answered wistfully. "Couldn't take my eyes off her at the spring dance. She caught me staring at her from across the table and smiled at me ever so faintly. I'll never forget that smile. Noelle was a wonderful person who gave me every bit of love she had. I tried to love her back. Truly, I did. But I had no love inside of me to give her. Noelle realized it soon enough and we went our separate ways. It was an amicable divorce, if such a thing is even . . ." He trailed off. Seemed far away for a moment. Then shook himself and said, "I owe it to Frances to head off this mess if I can. I owe it to Buzzy, too."

"You've heard that he tried to shoot himself yesterday?"

Luke Cahoon nodded his head sadly. "Poor Buzzy can't bear to go through it again either. He adored Frances."

"With all due respect, Congressman, your retirement won't head off our investigation."

"You'll do what you have to do," he acknowledged. "But at least the media won't bray quite so loudly if I step out of the picture. Besides, I've had it with the partisan blood sport in

Washington. I'm viewed as something of a hopeless old fuddy-duddy, you know, because I don't happen to consider the fellow who sits across the aisle from me to be Satan's spawn. I started serving in Congress because I wanted to fight for things. And I did fight for them. I brought jobs home to my district. I exposed tens of millions of dollars of fraud in our military procurement procedures. I've seen to the health needs of our combat veterans when not one of those armchair warriors on Capitol Hill gave a damn about them. When I saw a problem I tried to solve it. That's what the voters elect us to do. But Congress doesn't solve problems anymore. Now we *are* the problem."

"And so you're going to run away? I thought you were a fighter."

"I don't want to fight anymore. I'm all done fighting."

"I don't believe you, Congressman."

He shot an angry look at her. "Are you calling me a liar?"

"Let's just say I don't understand."

"And you never will. Not if I have anything to say about it. And I do."

CHAPTER 10

"MAKE SURE IT'S GOOD and taut, Mitch."

"Good and taut," he promised Bitsy, yanking hard on the orange string line. They were busy staking and measuring the site of his future patio. The day had turned overcast and raw. Gray clouds hung low over the waters of the sound, and the gulls were exceptionally vocal. Mitch drove the stake into the earth with a rubber mallet and stepped back to examine their work. "What do you think?"

"I think ten-by-twelve is too small," Bitsy responded, kneeling there in her overalls. "Let's try twelve-by-fourteen."

"Let's," he agreed. "Wait, do you have enough bluestone tucked away?"

"Oh, sure. I've got piles of leftovers. They won't all be the same size but we'll figure out a way to fit them together."

"Actually, I already have." The sketch he'd made was tucked in his jacket pocket. He unfolded it and showed it to her. "See, it's a sort of patchwork quilt pattern. With empty one-foot squares that'll be here, here and here. I can use these spaces for growing mint or thyme or whatever. Unless you think that would be too Martha Stewart-y. Why are you looking at me that way?"

Bitsy was gaping at him. "Sorry, I just . . . this is *beautiful*, Mitch. Did you design it all by yourself?"

"Not exactly."

"Oh, of course." She reached over and squeezed his hand. "It'll be a lovely tribute to her. I'll order a couple of yards of stone dust from Dorset Landscaping right away. Once we've laid a good level bed we'll fetch the stones from my place with your truck. Heck, we can knock this off in no time."

One thing Mitch had learned about Bitsy was that when it came to garden projects she did not dillydally around. Just marched right on over with her stakes, string lines and can-do spirit, raring to go. He'd been sprawled on his sofa with Clemmie and cup of hot cocoa watching one of Douglas Sirk's kitschiest 1950s masterpieces, *All That Heaven Allows*, a torrid tale of forbidden romance about a wealthy country club widow (Jane Wyman) and her *much* younger gardener (Rock Hudson). Mitch had felt a powerful urge to dive headfirst into Sirk ever since he'd had that cup of Postum yesterday at the club with the elegant Beryl Fairchild.

"Bitsy, what do you know about Bart Shaver?" he asked as they expanded the stake lines by two feet in each direction.

"He's a very nice boy. Buzzy doesn't deserve him."

"Okay, you'll have to explain that."

"Bart's decent and honorable, and from what I hear he wants to do good things with *The Gazette*. All Buzzy's ever done is shill for Bob Paffin and bore the hell out of people with that stupid 'Buzzings' column of his. As if anyone in town gives a hoot what that mean old man has to say about . . ." She broke off, puffing slightly. "I have a personal issue with Buzzy. I used to write the gardening column for *The Gazette*, you know."

"No, I didn't know."

"It was before you came to town. I had to give it up."

"Why?"

"Because Buzzy's behavior toward me was unacceptable. He was just unbelievably nasty. He hated my column. Hated all of my ideas for the paper. Hated having a *fee-male* in his precious newsroom. He has this stupid sign on the wall that says NO WHISTLING ALLOWED. It may as well say NO WOMEN. He's rude to all of the ladies. I am not a dog, Mitch. One day I finally told the old sourpuss that I was tired of being treated like one and I walked out. I've never been back since."

"I guess that explains it. . . ."

"Explains what?"

"Why Bart can't get the ladies in town to help him."

"You bet it does. We've staged a boycott."

"You said Buzzy hated your ideas for the paper. What sort of ideas?"

"Trend pieces about things that were going on in the community. Features that I thought would be of interest to mothers and daughters."

"I didn't know you were so interested in journalism."

"Young sir, I'll have you know that I was editor in chief of *The Sophian* my senior year at Smith. I had a reputation as something of a muckraker, too. When I sank my teeth in I wouldn't let go."

"My Aunt Myrna had a schnauzer just like that."

"Mitchell Berger, are you making fun of me?"

"Never."

"You'd better not be. Because I don't talk about this with most people."

"That's for sure. You've never said a word. How come?"

Bitsy gave the string line a tug. "Is your end good and taut?"

"Plenty good and taut. How come, Bitsy?"

"It's not something I'm proud of," she answered uncomfortably. "What I did after I graduated, I mean. I-I had this dream about moving to New York City and working on a fashion magazine. I wanted to be one of those chic young career girls who get to go to runway shows and offbeat art galleries. I wanted my own cute little apartment on the East Side. I wanted all of that. I even had a real shot at a job as assistant to the lady who was accessories editor at *Vogue*."

"Accessories are . . ."

"Handbags, gloves, that sort of thing. My English lit professor had been her roommate at Radcliffe. She wrote me a glowing letter of recommendation. I mailed it off to her friend at *Vogue*, who actually called me. We had a very nice chat on the phone and scheduled an interview at her office in the city later that week."

"And then what happened?"

Bitsy's face tightened. "I never went on the interview."

"You cancelled it?"

"Nothing quite so mature as that. I simply failed to show up."

"How come?"

"Because my parents were dead set against the idea of me working in the big, bad city. And they for darned sure didn't want me living there on my own. I didn't have the spine to stand up to them. So I caved. Ended up back here in Dorset as the assistant children's librarian. I spent three miserable years doing that until I married Redfield."

"Bitsy, I can't believe you never told me this before."

"What's to tell? It was a just a silly, stupid dream."

"Sorry, but you're talking to the wrong hombre. I don't think there's *anything* silly or stupid about dreams. You're also talking to someone who has a perfectly nice apartment in the city. It's not on the East Side, but it's plenty cute and you're plenty welcome to stay there any time you want."

She frowned at him, puzzled. "What would I do with myself?"

"Anything you want. Knock yourself out."

"You're very sweet, Mitch, but that particular dream died a long, long time ago. And I don't like to think about it. It just makes me sad when I do." Bitsy grabbed her rubber mallet and pounded the stake into the ground with great resolve. "Why did you ask me about Bart Shaver?"

"Because he's in desperate need of volunteers."

"I'm sure he is. But Bart won't get one woman in town to help him. Not while that cantankerous old man is still around."

Mitch heard the telephone ring inside of his house. He went in and answered it.

The voice on the other end said, "Mitch, this is Bart Shaver of *The Gazette* calling. I just moseyed over to the country club and had a nice long chat with Young Henry. Mind you, there's no such thing as a nice *short* chat with Young Henry. Do you know where the Cahoon family cemetery is?"

"No, I'm afraid not."

"It's on Johnny Cake Hill Road. Not far from the old Cahoon mansion at the top of the hill."

"Oh, sure, I know the place you mean. It's that pocket-sized cemetery hidden behind all of those bushes, right? I didn't realize it had a name."

"The Cahoons started burying their people up there way back in the 1600s—more than a hundred years before the town established Duck River Cemetery. There are a lot of Lays buried there, too. The two families intermarried early on. There's six other pre-Revolution family plots scattered throughout Dorset. Did you know that?"

"No, I didn't."

"It's fascinating stuff. I'll have to write a story about it one of these days. What makes the Cahoon family plot so unusual is that it's situated smack-dab in the middle of the club's seventh fairway. Or it would be if the designer hadn't figured out how to tuck it into its own little corner."

"You mean they had to build the golf course around it?"

"That's exactly what they had to do. Can you meet me up there in, say, an hour? I may have found what you're looking for."

Chapter 11

"You went *around* me, damn you!"

"Good morning to you, too, First Selectwoman." Des had just parked her cruiser in the lot behind Town Hall when the passenger door flew open and in jumped Glynis. "How are you today?"

"Don't you dare play dumb with me!" she roared, slamming the door shut behind her. "You have really pissed me off. And you do *not* want to piss me off."

"Yes, I can see that." What Des saw was a side of Glynis Fairchild-Forniaux she'd never witnessed before. Dorset's intensely driven first selectwoman had herself a serious temper. Her face was red. Her blues eyes were bulging. The lady looked deranged. Des wondered if this was a family trait. "Is there something in particular that I did?"

"You know there is. I expressly told you I wanted to be there when you spoke to my mother and you expressly ignored me."

"I haven't spoken to your mother, Glynis."

"No, you had your *boyfriend* do it. Talk about devious."

"Mitch goes his way, I go mine. And I think that pretty much wraps this up. Now if you'll please excuse me . . ."

Glynis didn't budge. Just sat there with her arms crossed

and her chin stuck out. "Damn it, Des, I thought we were on the same side."

"So did I."

"What's *that* supposed to mean?"

"It means you're the one who got miffy and uncooperative."

"When did I . . ."

"You told me I couldn't look at your father's personal papers without a judge's order."

"I'm a lawyer. What did you expect me to say?"

"That we've got ourselves a situation here and you'd do anything you could to help out."

Glynis softened slightly. "Okay, maybe I could have been a bit more accommodating."

"You think?"

"But I'll have to review them before I can let you have a look."

"Fair enough. How long will that take?"

"Two or three days."

"I haven't got two or three days."

The lady's eyes narrowed at her. "What's really going on, Des? I keep checking the Connecticut TV stations, the New London *Day, Hartford Courant.* All that they have is the same old story you people gave out yesterday about unidentified remains, possibly human. I deserve to know what's going on. My ass is in a sling here."

"I know it is."

"My project is a disaster. The entire historic district is one big ditch. Would you like to know how many angry voice mails I had when I got in this morning? Fifty-seven. I've got merchants, teachers, parents, *everyone* screaming at me. The only way this can get any worse is if it starts to rain. Then our kids will need kayaks to get to school."

Now that Glynis mentioned it the clouds overhead did seem to be getting grayer by the minute. Des glanced down at the weather app on her cell phone and said, "Actually, there's a 40 percent chance of widely scattered showers this afternoon—whatever that means."

Glynis sat there fuming. "My mother tells me that Buzzy Shaver spent the night up at Middlesex Hospital. It seems he tried to shoot himself yesterday, and might have succeeded if you hadn't managed to stop him. Des, *please* tell me what is happening."

"Fine. But this is just between us, hear me?"

"I hear you."

"We've confirmed that those are Lance Paffin's remains. The ME's preliminary findings are that he suffered a fatal wound to his skull from a spike-like object."

Glynis blinked at her. "Lance Paffin was murdered?"

"And buried under Dorset Street, which was undergoing regrading at the time. Then someone took the *Monster* out and wrecked her to make it look like he was lost at sea. His disappearance was a carefully hatched scheme. Your mother and father were among the last people to see him alive, along with the Paffins and Congressmen Cahoon. Exactly what has your mother told you about that night?"

"Very little," she said with a shake of her head. "Just that Lance was headstrong and foolish. Took his boat out when he shouldn't have and paid the price."

"How about your father? Did he ever talk about that night?"

"My father never talked about anything."

"Has your mother ever said anything else to you about Lance?"

"Such as what?"

"Whether she liked him, disliked him . . ."

"I've always had the impression that she was fond of everyone in the old gang. I know she's fond of Buzzy. He's not a strong person physically or emotionally. She worries about him." Glynis sat there in tightly coiled silence for a moment before she took a deep breath and said, "Okay, what am I missing here?"

"You won't enjoy hearing what I have to say."

"I don't care. Please tell me what you know."

"Lance Paffin was a major, major womanizer. I know that he slept with Delia before she married Bob. And with Buzzy's sister, Frances, who killed herself when Lance dumped her. Buzzy despised Lance for that, as did Luke Cahoon, who was engaged to marry Frances. I know that Lance slept with Helen Weidler and that he—"

"Wait, *my* Helen Weidler? I always thought Helen was a lifelong virgin."

"Think again." Des shoved her heavy horn-rimmed glasses up her nose and added, "I also know that he slept with your mother."

Glynis looked at her in disbelief. "My mother slept with Lance Paffin?"

"Yes."

"Was this before she married my father?"

"Well, yeah. Lance was dead and buried by then, remember?"

"Des, I-I don't . . ." All of the color had drained from Glynis's face. "I don't feel so good."

"If you're going to start blowing chunks please take it outside."

She reached for the door handle, then stopped, her hand wavering in midair. "No, I'm okay now. I had no idea that she . . . other than my father, you know?"

"I know," said Des, who felt no need to tell Glynis about her mother's trip to Barbados during spring break of her senior year at Wellesley. That was something for them to talk about between themselves. Or not. That was for Beryl to decide. "I've been trying, quietly and discreetly, to figure out what really happened to Lance that night."

Glynis looked at her searchingly. "And . . ."

"No one's talking. Not your mother. Not Buzzy. Not the Paffins. Not the congressman. Not anyone."

"So what happens next?"

"Quietly and discreetly go out the window and normal procedure takes over. And I don't just mean the Major Crime Squad. Lance was a naval officer. That means the feds will muscle in. And with the congressman in the middle of this it'll get huge."

Glynis considered this, her legal wheels starting to turn. "Maybe I should have a serious conversation with my mother."

Des's cell phone vibrated. It was the Deacon. She excused herself, stepped out of the vehicle and said, "What can I do for you, Daddy?"

"You can tell me what the congressman said to you this morning," he barked at her.

Instantly, she felt her stomach knot up. "Why are you asking me that?"

"Just answer the question, young lady."

"He said that he intends to announce his retirement from the US Congress later today, effective immediately." On the Deacon's chilly silence she said, "Okay, what's going on?"

"Not two minutes after you left him at the Fairburn Senior Center Congressman Cahoon ditched his staff *and* our escort cruiser and took off by himself in his Chevy Suburban."

"Took off for where?"

"I was hoping you'd tell me. How was he behaving?"

"He was defiant. Also quite bitter. He hates the idea that Frances Shaver's name will get dragged through the mud after all of these years. He never got over losing her. Or blaming Lance for it. He's hoping that if he resigns it'll take the media spotlight off of our investigation. He also told me he's sick of all of the partisan bickering in Washington, although I'm not sure I totally bought that." On the Deacon's continued chilly silence she added, "I was polite and respectful, if that's any comfort."

"It's not. Desiree, if you hear anything . . ."

"Not to worry. I'll Al Green you."

"You'll what?"

"I'll call you."

"Why didn't you just say so?" he muttered as rang off.

Des was just about to get back inside of her cruiser with Glynis when her cell phone vibrated again. This time the caller was Mitch. She took it. "What have you got for me? And please God make it good."

He said, "Listen, um, do you know the old Cahoon family cemetery at the top of Johnny Cake? . . ."

"I do," she replied, not liking the way his voice sounded. "What about it?"

"Bart Shaver asked me to meet him up here. And I just got here and he's lying f-face down in the grass. Somebody shot him in the back, Des. He's dead. Bart's dead."

The top of Johnny Cake Hill was the highest spot in the historic district and the site of Dorset's very first meetinghouse, according to the bronze plaque that had been installed there in 1949 by the historical society to commemorate its three hundredth anniversary. Johnny Cake Hill Road, which was steep and twisting, dead-ended at the oldest existing home in Dorset—the Thomas Cahoon House, a rambling, low-slung white Cape that dated back to 1647 and was the official residence of Congressman Luke Cahoon, who was presently among the missing.

Des saw no black Chevy Suburban in the congressman's driveway. No cars at all. And no lights were on in the house on this cloudy afternoon that seemed to be growing darker by the minute. The air felt extremely raw.

The house was surrounded by forty or so acres of woods. The Cahoon cemetery, which was officially the property of the town of Dorset, wasn't visible from the road. Mitch's old Studey truck was. It was snugged over onto the shoulder about a hundred yards down from the house, right behind a silver Honda Civic. Des noticed several sets of what appeared to be fresh tire prints in the moist earth behind the truck. She pulled onto the shoulder across the road so as not to disturb the tire prints and got out. A dense ten-foot-high thicket of wild blackberry, privet and forsythia shielded the cemetery from passersby. It was unmarked. If you didn't know it was there then you wouldn't know it was there. A narrow footpath snaked its way through the thicket. Des walked along the very edge of it to avoid compromising any shoe prints.

After about thirty feet the path arrived at the windswept little family cemetery, which enjoyed an incredible panoramic view of the mouth of the Connecticut River and Long Island Sound. Also of the seventh fairway of the country club's golf course, which lay just below it on the other side of an old, lichen-encrusted fieldstone wall. The cemetery was enclosed on all four sides by fieldstone walls. There were maybe a hundred gravestones. Most were of brownstone, which had been quarried plentifully in the area early on. Brownstone isn't as hard as granite or slate. The hand-carved inscriptions and elaborate images of skulls with wings had suffered serious erosion over the centuries. Many of the names, dates and biblical quotations were hard to make out. Some of the gravestones were rounded nubs no more than eight inches high. These marked the graves of small children and babies.

Bart Shaver lay dead on his stomach amidst the gravestones. Bart's left leg was straight, his right leg bent at the knee. Bart's head was turned so that it faced his bent knee. His eyes were open. On his face was a look of extreme disappointment. Des had never seen such a look of disappointment on the face of a dead man, and she'd seen a lot of dead men. And women. And children.

She would have to draw that look on Bart Shaver's dead face—assuming she ever figured out how to draw again.

He'd been shot three times in the back at very close range by what looked to be a .38. His tan herringbone-tweed blazer showed scorching and gunshot residue at the point of the entry wounds. Either someone had snuck up on Bart from behind or Bart had been talking to his shooter, then turned and started to walk away when the shooter opened fire. Des bent over and felt the exposed skin of his neck above the powder blue crewneck sweater he wore. Still a bit warm. It had happened within the past hour. She could see the bulge of Bart's wallet in the right rear pocket of his khaki trousers. It hadn't been a robbery, not that she for one second thought it had been. His cell phone lay in the grass next to his right knee.

Mitch stood a good distance away from Bart intently studying a gravestone, his hands buried in the pockets of his olive green C. C. Filson wool jacket, a manila folder tucked under one arm. He hadn't acknowledged her arrival. Hadn't so much as looked at her. Or Bart. Wouldn't. Couldn't.

She phoned it in. A trooper from Troop F in Westbrook would be there soon to provide backup. Within twenty minutes the crime-scene techies and the ME's death investigator would arrive, followed soon thereafter by officers from the Major Crime Squad. There was no avoiding them now.

She approached Mitch, moving her way slowly toward him.

"Have you ever been up here before?" he asked her, his hollow-eyed gaze never leaving the inscribed gravestone. "Check this out . . . Titus Cahoon, deceased on the 27th of

May, 1719, at the age of seventy. He was born here in 1649. Lived his entire life here two whole generations before the American Revolution, can you imagine? And get a look at Elijah Lay over here. . . . Elijah was a Revolutionary War hero. Served in the Eighth Company, Sixth Regiment. Died April 4, 1818 at the age eighty-one. Isn't that incredible?"

"Incredible," she said patiently. He was inching his way closer to Bart's body. He'd get there when he was ready to get there.

"And, look, there's *eight* kids buried here, aged five and younger, who all died within a few months of each other in 1696." The tiny gravestones were clustered close together and surrounded by a low, spiked wrought-iron fence. "There must have been a smallpox or diphtheria outbreak." He edged his way still closer to Bart, looking up at her now for the first time. "He's in half-frog pose."

"He's in what?"

"That's a yoga pose he's doing. My teacher, Liza, likes to call it roadkill pose. It's a hip and groin opener. I find it also works on the piriformis muscles in my butt, which are always tight because I sit on them so much. Do you think he'll be given a proper burial?"

"Bart? Sure, he will."

"I meant Lance Paffin."

She studied him as they stood there together in the light drizzle that was starting to fall. "Are you okay, baby?"

"Not really."

"Want to tell me what happened?"

"I got him killed. That's what happened. It's my fault."

"Why do you say that?"

"Because I asked him to look into something for me. Actually, I didn't ask him. He volunteered. He was hoping I'd do him a solid in return."

"What did you ask him to look into?"

Mitch didn't answer her.

"Baby, what's in that folder under your arm?"

Again, he didn't answer. Just gazed at her with those sad-puppy eyes of his. "What we're into here, this is *not* a Douglas Sirk movie, you know? There are no violins playing. No pretty people. And the color palette is just way off. The bloodstains on his back don't even match the color of his sweater."

"Don't match the what?"

"I have to go now," he announced abruptly.

"Mitch, we have to talk about this."

"Can't right now. Can't be here. I only stayed because I didn't want the poor guy to be all alone."

Des put her hand on his arm. "Okay, we'll talk later," she said gently.

Mitch didn't hear her. He'd already started toward the fieldstone wall that protected the little cemetery from the golf course. He climbed over it and began his way across the seventh fairway, walking stiffly like a zombie. She would have gone after him except she couldn't leave the murder scene. Besides, he needed some time alone to process his horror. He'd be okay.

And she had something she needed to do before the others arrived. Des always kept a fresh latex glove in her jacket pocket. Quickly, she put it on, snatched up Bart's cell phone from the grass and checked his call log. The young journalist had placed two calls in the last hour of his life. One was to Mitch's home number. He'd called someone else ten minutes after that. She stared at that person's name and number before setting the phone back down exactly where she'd found it.

She was pocketing the glove when the trooper from the Troop F barracks arrived. She instructed him to cordon off the perimeter a hundred feet down Johnny Cake Hill Road. While he did that she strode up to Congressman Cahoon's house for a closer look around. The black Suburban wasn't in his garage. Just an old silver Mercedes 450SL two-seater convertible. She knocked on the front door. No one answered. She peered inside a front window. Saw nothing and no one. Strode around the immaculately manicured grounds to the back of the house and peered in the French doors to the kitchen. Still saw nothing and no one. No lights were on anywhere.

She started back toward the cemetery now, reaching for her cell phone. When he picked up she said, "Daddy, this one's turned hot. Buzzy Shaver's young cousin, Bart, has just been shot dead in the Cahoon family cemetery at the top of Johnny Cake Hill. It's adjacent to the congressman's home."

The Deacon was silent for a long moment before he said, "Is the congressman home?"

"Doesn't appear to be—unless he ditched the Suburban and is hiding in the dark. I can no longer keep it quiet. I've called in the Major Crime Squad."

"As well you should," he stated stiffly. "Thank you for alerting me. Please call if you have anything else to tell me."

"I will."

"Desiree? . . ." He fell silent again. She could practically feel him struggling for the words. Feelings were not his thing. "I'm sorry about this."

"Me, too. There's a big supply of sorry to go around."

By now the crime-scene technicians were pulling up in their blue-and-white cube vans, followed by the death investigator. Soon after that a two-woman team in dark-colored pantsuits arrived from the Major Crime Squad. The lead investigator was Des's protégé and friend Yolanda Snipes, an exceptionally fierce half-black, half-Cuban pit bull with breasts who'd fought her way out of Hartford's Frog Hollow projects to make it all of the way to lieutenant. Her pint-sized young sergeant was Toni Tedone, who was 70 percent big hair and 30 percent hooters. Toni the Tiger was one of the Waterbury Mafia Tedones—the clan of Italian-Americans from the Brass City who pretty much ran the state police. Back before a case blew up in Des's face, back when it was *she* who was a lieutenant handling homicides, her sergeant had been Toni's chesty, fathead cousin Rico. Now Rico was on the Drug Task Force and it was little Toni who'd been handed a choice slot on the Major Crime Squad. Toni was a first of, as in the first member of the Waterbury Mafia who was a she.

When Yolie saw Des standing there her scarred face broke into a big smile. "Hey, Miss Thing."

"Hey back at you. I thought that you girls were busy."

Yolie let out a laugh. "That's a US congressman's house over there, am I right? Guess what? We are suddenly unbusy."

"How are you, Yolie?"

"Always happy to see you."

"Me, too," exclaimed Toni, who surprised the hell out of Des by giving her a great big oofy hug. "You're looking *fabulous*."

"Why, thank you," Des responded, taking notice of the new, size-huge diamond engagement ring Toni was sporting on her left ring finger.

"Who is our victim, Miss Thing?"

"Bart Shaver of *The Gazette*. He was shot three times in the back from very close range by what looks to me like a .38. But what do I know?"

"More than I ever will. Bag and tag the victim's cell phone, Sergeant. And go have a look-see in his car."

"Right, Loo. And his keys are . . ."

"It'll be unlocked," Des said. "No one ever locks their cars in Dorset."

"Oh, right, I forgot. This is the sweet little place where nothing ever happens. Am I look-seeing for anything in particular?"

"He was a reporter," Des said. "I'd grab his laptop if it's there. Also any five-by-eight notepads you might find."

"And canvass the neighbors down the road," Yolie told her. "Find out if they heard the shots or saw somebody driving away. This is a dead-end road. There can't be too many cars coming and going."

"On it, Loo."

Des eyed Toni curiously as she marched off, her little arms pumping.

"She's taking a cruise on The Love Boat," Yolie explained, following Des's gaze.

"Who's the lucky fellow?"

"You know Vicki Dmytryk, that tall, blond district prosecutor?"

"Sure. Vicki has a brother, Bill, who's in private practice. I tangled with him in court once. So she and Bill hooked up?"

"Guess again."

Des frowned at her for a second before she said, "Wait, no way. . . ."

Yolie nodded solemnly. "Yes way."

"Did you ever—"

"Not even maybe. All she'd ever told me was that she was tired of her uncles fixing her up with every unattached Italian-American man in the department."

"And now we know why. Does her family know she and Vicki are engaged?"

"She hasn't worked up the nerve to tell them yet. And they aren't engaged, technically. That's a promise ring she's wearing. It's like an agreement to agree or something. I don't quite get it, but don't go by me. I haven't been on a date in eleven months. And he bailed on me during the salad course."

"You were too much woman for him, Yolie."

"I'm too much something," she sighed, glancing at the death investigator who was crouched over Bart Shaver's body. "Anything funky I should know?"

"Actually, we do have a situation here."

"Is that right? Why is it that I never, ever hear the word 'situation' in connection with anything I'm going to like?"

"I can pretty much guarantee you won't like this. Allow me to hit rewind. A paving crew unearthed a set of human skeletal remains under Dorset Street yesterday morning.

Possibly you noticed the tent and the ME's crew when you drove by?"

"Sure did. Whose remains are they?"

"US Navy Lt. Lance Paffin, the older brother of our former first selectman, Bob."

"Who is a total weasel if I'm remembering right."

"You're remembering right. Supposedly, Lance disappeared at sea off of his catboat, the *Monster*, in May of 1967 after a night of carousing at the country club over yonder with friends. Bob and his future bride, Delia, were there. So were Chase Fairchild and his future bride, Beryl, the parents of our current first selectwoman. And so was our soon-to-be-former Congressman Luke Cahoon. But as we now know—"

"Wait, did you just say our soon-to-be-*former* congressman?"

"I did. And I'll get to that in a sec. We now know that Lance was never lost at sea. He's been underneath Dorset Street this whole time. According to the ME, he suffered a fatal blow to the cranium from a spike-like object of some kind. Somebody murdered him. Somebody buried him. And somebody took the *Monster* out and left it adrift out there. The Coast Guard found it washed up on the rocks at Saybrook Point the following morning. No sign of Lance. An extensive search was conducted but his body was never found. Until yesterday, that is, when a road crew dug up the pavement on Dorset Street for the first time since May of 1967. It has needed regrading for years but Bob Paffin was always vehemently opposed to it—supposedly for financial reasons. And he had the strong editorial backing of our shooting victim's elderly cousin, Clyde 'Buzzy' Shaver, who's the editor and publisher of *The Gazette* as well as Bob's lifelong friend.

It also might interest you to know that Buzzy tried to shoot his own face off yesterday with a deer rifle. I managed to talk him out of it."

"Damn, girl, you've been busy."

"Just a typical day in the life a small town resident trooper," Des said as they stood there in what now qualified as more than a light drizzle. The techies had put on rain slickers.

Yolie glowered up at the sky. "Was it supposed to rain today?"

"Forty percent chance of widely scattered showers."

"Somebody gets *paid* to make that shit up? I want *his* job." She studied Des, her brown eyes narrowing. "So what's the up?"

"The up is that the people who were the last ones to see Lance alive concocted an elaborate fable about what happened to him. They've been living with that fable for a long, long time. And now . . ."

"They've got some explaining to do," Yolie said, nodding her head.

"As do we, I'm sorry to say. We dropped the ball on this one, Yolie. It was winky-wink from start to finish. We cut a bunch of shmancy country club blue bloods way too much slack. All of them had been drinking heavily. And I'm told there was a pretty heated quarrel out in the parking lot. Something happened that night. But the investigators who followed up *didn't* follow up. No one was questioned any further. Not Lance's friends. Not the club staff. Not anyone who worked at or lived near the yacht club. Fingerprint evidence that was taken from the boat's tiller somehow went missing. And our lead investigator somehow ended up with a sweet job as chief of staff for soon-to-be Congressman Luke Cahoon. The media will go nutcakes with this one when the details come out. And they will come out."

Yolie shrugged her bulked up weightlifter's shoulders. "Ancient history. Who cares?"

"The Deacon cares."

Her face dropped. "Oh, so it's like that."

"Yes, it's like that. Just between us? He got the ME's findings yesterday afternoon. He's been slow walking them to your squad commander to give me a window of time before this whole thing explodes in our faces."

"So what are you telling me?" Yolie demanded, her nostrils flaring. "You've been running your own one-girl murder squad?"

"That's correct." Des braced herself for an explosion. Yolie was uber-turfy.

But she merely nodded her head and said, "Whatever."

Des looked at her in disbelief. "You're okay with it?"

"Oh, hell no," she said calmly. "But it is what it is. And this is me rolling with it. I had what you'd call an epiphany a few weeks ago. And I have Toni to thank for it. Know what she told me? That I'm a miserable person to be stuck in a car with because I wake up pissed off at the world and I stayed pissed off all day and night. And that if I don't figure out how to be happy I won't ever be able to make anyone else happy—like, say, a man."

"Toni said that?"

"Girl dealt me some pretty serious wisdom. I took it to heart. Some days I do pretty good at it, too."

"And other days?"

"I still just want to punch somebody's face in." Yolie thumbed her chin thoughtfully. "You *are* going to share what you found out, aren't you?"

"Of course. Lance was someone who had many, many enemies—the reason being that he boinked *everyone*. The man was an equal opportunity hound. He boinked brother Bob's fiancée, Delia. He boinked our first selectwoman's mother, Beryl. Got her pregnant even. He also boinked Luke Cahoon's fiancée, Frances Shaver, kid sister of Buzzy. When Lance dumped Frances she killed herself. Neither the congressman nor Buzzy ever got over it. When I spoke to the congressman this morning about Frances he went four paws up on me. Told me he intends to retire from the US Congress today at 5 PM because he can't bear to have her name dragged through the mud again."

"And are you buying into that?"

"Oh, hell no. As soon as I left him the congressman ditched his aides and took off. His present whereabouts are unknown. And now Buzzy Shaver's young cousin Bart has three fresh holes in his back."

"What do you know about him?"

Des glanced over at Bart, her chest tightening. "I know that he took what he did seriously. He even tried to go after Bob Paffin for being a corrupt dirtbag until Buzzy shut him down. Bob's been quietly keeping *The Gazette* afloat financially. Or I should say he was. As soon as the voters gave him the boot he pulled the plug on Buzzy, which means *The Gazette* has to go entirely digital next month. It's Bart who's been making that happen. Buzzy's still a card-carrying member of the manual-typewriter generation. Plus he has major emphysema."

"Any idea what Bart was doing here in this old cemetery?"

"All I know is he phoned Mitch and asked Mitch to meet him here."

"Yeah, I saw your boy's truck." Yolie looked around, frowning. "Where is he?"

"He went wandering off across the seventh fairway. Told me this was all his fault. I have no idea what he meant. He wasn't ready to talk about it."

"Was Buzzy Shaver partying at the club the night Lance disappeared?"

"I'm told not. He had to stay home and take care of his mother."

"Yet as soon as Lance's remains are found he tries to blow his face off. And the congressman suddenly decides to retire. And now we've got us a shooting victim and there's no way Bart's death isn't tied in with whatever happened to Lance forty-seven years ago. Or am I missing something?"

"You're not missing a thing."

"And you weren't kidding, Miss Thing. We've got us a situation." Yolie mulled it over. "For starters, we'd better find our missing congressman. Are you sure he's not home?"

"No, I'm not sure. He could be hiding out. But I didn't have just cause to break down his door."

"Leave that to me. We need to find out where he's been for the past hour. Same goes for the rest of your blue-blooded Depends set. We have to account for everybody's whereabouts."

Toni came marching back toward them now, her little arms still pumping. "Victim's car is clean, Loo," she reported. "No laptop. No notepads. I haven't found a neighbor yet who heard or saw a thing. But a lot of folks aren't home right now. I can try them again later."

Yolie looked at Des. "Any other ideas?"

"I thought I saw fresh tire prints out there. But maybe those belong to someone who visited a loved one here today. Maybe the shooter cut across that fairway on foot and left the scene by way of the club's parking lot. If so, he or she may have been observed by someone in the club. For that matter, he or she may be hiding in plain sight by eating lunch there as we speak."

Yolie nodded. "Sergeant, you'll want to write down the names of everyone who signed in at the club today."

"Will do, Loo."

"Want me to notify the next of kin?" Des asked.

"That would be great."

Not to mention easy. Her cell rang at that very moment. It was Buzzy Shaver.

He wheezed in her ear before he said, "Resident Trooper Mitry? I was wondering if you could swing by the newsroom. There are some folks here who'd like to speak with you."

"I'll be right there, Mr. Shaver." She rang off and said, "After you girls get things buttoned up here you may want to meet me at offices of *The Gazette* on Dorset Street."

Yolie peered at Des curiously. "Real, what's going on?"

"Real, I have no idea."

As Des went striding out of the old cemetery she tried calling Mitch on his cell. He didn't pick up. She texted him the 411 on where she was heading. Then she jumped into her cruiser and took off.

CHAPTER 12

MITCH DIDN'T FEEL A thing as he staggered his way across the seventh fairway in the chilly drizzle. His feet were numb. His legs seemed to be operating under their own power. And his head wasn't even in Dorset at all. It was back at another old cemetery, the one in Stockbridge, Massachusetts, where Maisie had been laid to rest on that bright, crisp fall morning. She'd been a Lawrenson, and all of the Lawrensons were buried in a family plot that was a stone's throw from the fabled Sedgwick Pie, where the ancestors of Edie Sedgwick, the Andy Warhol superstar, could be found. The gravestones in that cemetery had been slate, not brownstone. And there were maple leaves on the ground that morning. The color of the fallen leaves matched the hand-knit shawl that Maisie's sister, Gretchen, had been wearing over her black dress.

Now *that* was genuine Douglas Sirk.

As Mitch made his way across the fairway, dazed, he felt as if he were right back there again with his grief and his utter aloneness. Maisie's mom shooting hard, narrow looks at him. Her dad refusing to look at him at all—as if Maisie's death from ovarian cancer was somehow *his* fault. As if Maisie would still be alive if she'd married someone else. Someone who wasn't a fat Jewish movie critic from New York City whose grandparents had arrived in America by way of Ellis Island and Orchard Street.

I didn't kill her.

That was what he kept wanting to tell Mrs. Lawrenson. Even though she wouldn't speak to him before or after the ceremony. Even though part of him—a mighty big part—did blame himself. Because he wasn't able to stop it from happening.

I didn't kill her.

But I did kill Bart Shaver.

And there was no way he would ever stop blaming himself. Not for as long as he lived.

Eventually, his feet delivered him down the cart path to the head groundskeeper's building, which was tucked behind a fence near the third green. It was a combination office, tool shed and garage. A dump truck was parked outside of the open garage door, along with two big rider mowers and a golf cart that had been converted for utility duty. Inside, the garage was crammed with a number of smaller mowers as well as whackers, trimmers, edgers, spreaders and leaf blowers. Huge bags of grass seed, fertilizer, sand and assorted weed-killing agents were stacked high on wooden pallets.

Two middle-aged guys in overalls were in the process of taking a mower apart on the floor of the garage. Make that one of them was taking it apart. The other was consulting the service manual and cursing a lot.

An open doorway connected the garage to the office, where an elderly man was seated at a cluttered desk poring over a seed catalogue. A potbellied stove was going in the corner of the cozy office. Mitch made his way over toward it. He hadn't realized it but he was shivering from the cold.

"Hello, they-yah, young fella," the old man exclaimed with the salty Rhode Island inflection that Mitch occasionally heard come from the mouths of Dorset's older working people. "Something I can do for you? Or did you just come in to warm your bones?"

"I was . . . looking for Young Henry." Mitch's own voice sounded rusty.

"And you found him." Young Henry had to be pushing eighty, although he still seemed ruddy and plenty fit in his checked wool shirt, moleskin trousers and well-worn work boots. Alert, too. His blue eyes were piercing and sharp. He had big ears, a big, bony nose and huge brown hands that were roughened from a lifetime of outdoor work. "You're not a member, are you? I'm pretty sure I know all of the club members."

"My name's Mitch. I'm a friend of Bart Shaver."

"Is that right? Afraid you missed him. Bart was hee-yah, oh, must be an hour ago." He peered at Mitch curiously. "Say, you don't look so hot, you don't mind me saying so. Kind of on the pale side. Are you okay?"

"Define . . . okay."

"Park yourself there, son," he commanded him, gesturing to an old easy chair next to the stove. "Have just the thing for you. Got a quarter?"

"A quarter? . . ."

"Never you mind. It's my treat." Young Henry sprang nimbly to his feet and went over to a battered red Coca-Cola vending machine—a boxy floor-chest model that had to be fifty years old. He fished a couple of quarters out of his trouser pocket, popped them into the coin slot and, raised the lid. Removed two chilled six-and-a-half-ounce glass bottles and lowered the lid. Opened them with the opener that was fixed to the side of the chest, handed Mitch one and sat back down with the other. "Now you drink that whole thing right down," he ordered Mitch. "It'll put the color back in your cheeks."

Mitch gulped it down. He didn't usually care much for soda pop but he had to admit that this particular bottle of icy cold Coke tasted awfully damned good. Also that its infusion of corn syrup, caffeine and god-knows-what-else perked him up almost instantly.

"Doesn't taste any good unless it's in a glass bottle," Old Henry informed him, sipping his leisurely.

"I thought they stopped making these little glass bottles last year."

"Yes, sir, they did."

"Wait, don't tell me. You have a ten-year supply of them stashed somewhere, don't you?"

Young Henry didn't say. Just smiled at him. "Mind you, the glass isn't near as thick as it used to be in the old days. But that's life. You have to make do. We've had that machine since the early sixties. Used to be by the swimming pool until the club decided to install the snack bar. They wanted us to get rid of it. Dad said to them, heck, I'll take it. And darned if it doesn't still run. That's because they built things to last in those days. Would you believe that the compressor on the last refrigerator the wife and I bought crapped out in less than five years? Plus the danged thing never did keep my bee-yah cold enough."

Mitch warmed his hands over the stove, gazing around at the homey office. There seemed to be duck decoys and fishing rods everywhere. An old wall clock was tick-tocking away. It felt as if the old man's whole life had been lived in this office, *tick-tock, tick-tock*. He was totally at ease here, *tick-tock, tick-tock*.

"Feel better now?" he asked, eyeing Mitch critically.

"Much better, thanks."

"Did you pick up a bug or something?"

"No, I'm just having a really rotten day," Mitch said. "Forgive me for staring, but when I heard that your name was Young Henry I was expecting—"

"Someone young?" He cackled in amusement. "Well, I *was* young, once upon a time. And when I first came to work hee-yah they took to calling me Young Henry so as to tell me apart from my dad, who also went by the name of Henry. He was the original head groundskeeper when this club first opened back in 1936—which also so happens to be when I was born."

"So that would make you . . ."

"Seventy-eight years old," he said. "You got something against older people working?"

"No, sir. Not a thing."

"What would I do with myself all day if I didn't work? Sit around on my keester watching Movies on Demand on the TV?"

"No, sir. Besides, I don't need the competition."

"You don't need the what?"

"Nothing. Don't mind me."

"My dad put me to work hee-yah part time way back when I was still in high school. I hired on full time soon as I finished my schooling. When he retired back in 1972 I took over for him. Only job I've ever had. Or wanted."

"And is there a next-generation Henry learning the ropes from you?"

"Afraid not. Our two girls both married paper pushers. And our grandsons don't seem to care about a thing except for those handheld computer games of theirs. Always pushing the little buttons with their thumbs like lab monkeys. I can barely get them to talk to me. But I've got a couple of good young fellas I'm bringing along," he said, meaning the middle-aged guys who were servicing the mower out in the garage. "And I have no intention of retiring any time soon. I've don't need glasses or a hearing aid. And my doctor says he wishes *his* cholesterol and blood pressure were as low as mine. I get plenty of fresh air and exercise. I never smoked. Never drank anything stronger than bee-yah. I figure I should be good for another ten years easy." He took another sip of his Coke, eyeing Mitch with those piercing blue eyes. "Bart's a good kid. Buzzy's lucky to have him."

"Do you mind if I ask you what you and he talked about?"

"Don't know if I do or I don't." Young Henry tilted his head at Mitch slightly. "Why are you asking?"

"He's been helping me collect some background information. We're working on a story together for *The Gazette*."

"Uh-huh. So why don't you talk to *him* about it?"

"That's not possible right now."

"Uh-huh. Well, no harm in repeating myself, I guess. Seems like I do it all the time whether I intend to or not—or so the wife says. Bart was asking me about that old spiked fence we used to have around the rose garden before the big fire of '92."

Mitch opened the manila folder he was toting and removed Bob and Delia Paffin's wedding photograph. "Do you mean this fence?"

Young Henry squinted at it. "Yep, that's the one. Can't understand why the both of you are so curious about it. Hasn't been they-yah since the ladies on the garden committee decided they wanted a boxwood hedge instead. Bart wondered if I had the vaguest idea where it might be these days. I told him I don't have the vaguest idea at all. I know exactly where it is. Moved it they-yah myself." He drained his bottle of Coke, smacking his lips together with pleasure. "Care for another, son? This one will cost ya."

"I'm just fine, thanks. Moved it where?"

"To the Cahoon family cemetery up by our seventh fairway. Dorset's cemetery commission is supposed to be responsible for the upkeep of the old family plots that are tucked around town, but most of the actual work gets done by volunteers from the VFW and the Boys Scouts. I take care of the Cahoon cemetery. Always have. It's the neighborly thing to do. Some of those old gravestones are getting so crumbly I'm afraid they'll turn to dust if I bump my mower into them. There's one particular cluster of real early children's gravestones, tiny ones, that's in sad shape. That's where I put the fence. I felt those little 'uns ought to be protected. Thought it looked kind of nice there, too."

"This would be those kids who died in 1696?"

Young Henry frowned at him. "Sounds to me like you already knew the answer to your question."

"Just making sure."

"That's it, all right." He peered at the photo again. "This is Bob and Delia's wedding, isn't it?"

"Yes, sir. I guess you're a bit older than they are."

Young Henry nodded. "Five, six years."

"That would make you about the same age as Bob's brother Lance."

"Just about. Lance was one class ahead of me."

"What did you think of him?"

"Think of him?" He let loose with another cackle of laughter. "Lance was *the* wildest young buck Dorset's ever seen. That fella couldn't get enough of women—I am talking two, three different women a day, seven days a week, fifty-two weeks a year. He wanted them all. And they all wanted him. Even the married ones who should have known better. Why, he could turn even the most prim and proper ones into shameless hussies. One Sunday morning—and I'll never forget this for as long as I live—I came in hee-yah real early to get some mowing done for my dad. This was back in, let's see, the summer of '62 it was. There'd been a luau party here the night before or some such. Anyhow, I'm walking by the pool and what do I see but Lance and another man's pretty blond wife fast asleep together on a couple mats, naked as can be. I couldn't believe what I was seeing. I woke those two up and told them in no uncertain terms to get their clothes on and get the hell out. This hee-yah is a nice club for nice people, not a brothel. She was awful ashamed. As well she should have been, her not only being married but a good fif-teen years older than Lance. She couldn't get dressed and run fast enough. But Lance was as cool as can be. Offered me fifty dollars cash money to keep my mouth shut. 'Here's something for your trouble, sport,' was what he said. Which I didn't care for one bit. Don't ever call me 'sport.'"

"I won't."

"I told him to keep his money."

"Did you ever tell anyone what you saw?"

"Not a soul. Not my dad. And for danged sure not the wife. She's a devout Christian and would have insisted I speak up. But I figured what people want to do is their own business. Besides which, I didn't want that particular married lady for an enemy." Young Henry sat back in his chair with a sigh. "Lance always gave me a sneaky smile after that, like him and me played for the same team."

"And how about the married lady?"

"Couldn't look me in the eye. She'd scurry off soon as she saw me coming."

"What do you think happened to Lance on the night he disappeared?"

"Why, he took the *Monster* out and fell overboard. Every-one knows that."

"Everyone doesn't know that he was found buried under Dorset Street yesterday morning in his dress blues."

Young Henry's eyes widened. "Is that why they stopped the dig?"

"It is."

"He's been under the road this whole time?"

Mitch nodded. "With a fractured skull."

"Say, you must be the Mitch who keeps company with our resident trooper."

"It's true, I am."

"Is she figuring that somebody *murdered* Lance?"

"It certainly appears that way."

Young Henry tugged at a big ear. "Holy Toledo. . . ."

"Do you have any idea who might have wanted him dead?"

"You mean other than half of the men in Dorset? The way Lance went through women *somebody* was bound to go after him eventually. He was asking for it." Young Henry handed the Paffins' wedding photo back to Mitch and said, "When I told Bart where he could find this hee-yah fence he ran out that door like a bat out of hell. I wouldn't be surprised if that's where you'll find him right this very minute."

"I wouldn't be surprised either." Mitch's cell phone vibrated in his pocket. He reached for it, glancing down at its screen. Des was texting him her next destination. He pocketed it, running a hand through his damp, unruly curls. "Why didn't you want her for an enemy?"

Young Henry frowned at him. "Who's this we're talking about now?"

"The married lady who you found by the pool with Lance."

"Oh, her." His weathered face dropped. "Because she was in a position to get me fired if she decided I was going to cause trouble for her."

"Trouble with her husband, you mean?"

"That, too."

"There was some other kind?"

"Oh, most definitely."

"Would you mind elaborating on that?"

"I don't mind. See, it so happens that the lady in question was also the mother of one of Lance's own friends."

"You don't say."

"I do. I do say."

Mitch leaned forward, his pulse quickening. "Which friend?"

CHAPTER 13

SEVERAL CARS WERE PARKED in the damp, creosote-scented
dirt road outside of the office of *The Gazette*. And when Des
went inside she found the newsroom crowded with people,
most of them over the age of seventy. Bob and Delia Paffin
were standing there, both wearing raincoats and tense expres-
sions. The missing congressman, Luke Cahoon, was there,
looking grave and statesmanlike. Beryl Fairchild was there,
looking cool and calm. So was her daughter, who looked
anything but. Glynis was pacing back and forth, back and
forth.

Buzzy Shaver was seated in a swivel chair in front of his
enormous rolltop desk wearing a white button-down shirt,
dark green knit tie and gray slacks. There was a nearly full
bottle of Old Overholt rye whiskey and a shot glass on the
desk next to his vintage manual typewriter. Also a laptop that
looked an awful lot like Bart's laptop. A half dozen five-by-
eight notepads were stacked on top of it. In his right hand
Buzzy was holding a Ruger Speed Six revolver, a circa-seventies
six-shooter that had a short barrel and a round, compact grip.
The Ruger wasn't much for long-range accuracy but for close-
up work it did just fine. Fired a .38 Smith and Wesson cartridge if Des's memory served her right. And it did.

Buzzy wasn't pointing it at anyone. Just sitting there holding it in the palm of his hand, his moist, pendulous lower lip stuck out peevishly.

"Want to give me that gun?" Des asked him, breaking the taut silence in the newsroom.

"I don't think so," the old editor wheezed in response. "Although you're welcome to try and take it from me."

"Is that some kind of a dare?"

Buzzy didn't answer her. Just poured himself a jolt of Old Overholt and drank it down while the others stood there in stiff silence.

"I'm sorry to disappoint you, Mr. Shaver, but if you're angling for an officer-assisted suicide you picked the wrong trooper. Also the wrong day. Yesterday, I felt genuine sympathy for you. Today, you can go ahead and blow your miserable head off for all I care."

"That was your big mistake," he said, gazing down at the Ruger in his hand. "You shouldn't have talked me out of it."

"Don't you put any of this on me. And don't bother trying to play with my head. I won't lose my temper and shoot you. Not going to happen. I have a lot more experience at this sort of thing than you do. Just for starters, I know that you're not going to shoot yourself. Not in front of all of these nice ladies. So why don't you just put the gun down, okay? You and I both know that you won't be using it again."

"*Again?*" Glynis looked at her sharply. "What is that supposed to mean?"

"Somebody shot Bart Shaver to death in the Cahoon family cemetery about an hour ago."

Glynis let out a gasp. Her mother and the others merely

stood there stone-faced. They already knew. Of course they did.

"Bart was shot three times in the back from very close range with a .38. His killer took Bart's laptop and notepads." Des gestured at Buzzy's desk. "That laptop and those note-pads, unless I'm wrong. And I'm not. Have you fired that gun recently, Mr. Shaver?"

"You know I have."

"I don't know a damned thing." Des looked around at the group of old friends who were gathered there. "For instance, why are all of you here?" On their total silence she gazed at Dorset's former first selectman and said, "How about it, Bob?"

"Beryl phoned me and asked me to come here," he answered quietly.

"And what about you, Congressman? I heard you rabbited on your staff after I left you in Fairburn."

"I needed to be alone for a while, Master Sergeant," Luke Cahoon said, gazing down his long nose at her. "Senior centers happen to depress the hell out of me. It's the smell of all of that perfume, chiefly. It reminds me of funeral parlors. So I got the hell away from there. I do have that right, you know. If I feel like going somewhere, I go somewhere."

"And where did you go?"

"Are you *questioning* me?"

"Have you been to your house up on Johnny Cake Hill Road?"

"The congressman was at my house," Bob interjected. "We were in my study having a highball when Beryl called. He and I drove here together."

"So I'll find your black Suburban at the Paffin place?" she asked the congressman.

"*Yes*, you'll find it there," he answered with elaborate patience.

Des turned to Delia Paffin. "And you were where?"

"Grocery shopping at the A&P. Bob reached me on my cell phone after he heard from Beryl, and I met him here. Him and Luke, that is to say. I still have the groceries outside in my car. And my receipt, which is time-stamped. And you can ask the cashier, Rosie, if you don't believe me."

"I didn't say I didn't believe you."

"You didn't have to," Delia huffed, her plump cheeks mottling. "I can see it in those eyes of yours."

Des looked at Glynis now. "And you're here because—"

"You phoned me and suggested I meet you here. I'm grateful that you did, Des."

"No problem. You told me you wanted to be in the loop. Welcome to the loop." Next Des turned to Beryl Fairchild and said, "Why did you phone Bob?"

Beryl glanced over at Buzzy, who continued to sit there at his desk chair, Ruger in hand, glowering. "I stopped by here to look in on Buzzy," she explained in a soft voice. "I'm the one who brought him home from the hospital this morning, you see. Once I got him settled there I left to run some errands. I tried phoning him a while later to see how he was doing but he didn't answer. After I'd tried him several times I got a bit concerned so I drove to his house. He wasn't home. I thought he might have come here. I didn't see his car parked out front but I came inside anyway to see if Bart knew where he was."

"Bart's car was here?"

"No, but he likes . . . liked to ride his bike to work. Only, Bart wasn't here either. No one was. The place was deserted."

"And the office door was unlocked?"

"We never lock this newsroom during business hours," Buzzy informed her. "It's a family tradition. My father never locked it. And my grandfather never locked it. If anyone has a story for us they can just walk right in, whether someone's here or not. That's one tradition my ball boy didn't dare trample on. Besides, there's nothing around here worth stealing."

"Not even that Ruger of yours?"

He glanced down at his gun. "This I keep locked in the bottom drawer of my desk, along with a bottle of the good stuff. Also a family tradition."

"I was going to leave a note on Buzzy's desk asking him to please call me," Beryl went on, "when he suddenly came bursting in the door with that—that gun in his hand."

"Did he say anything to you about Bart?"

"He didn't say anything to me at all. He was having trouble breathing."

"How about the laptop and notepads? Did he have those with him when he came in the door?"

Beryl lowered her blue eyes, swallowing. "I don't recall."

"You're a lousy liar, ma'am."

"I sat him down right there and made him use his inhaler. Then I poured him a stiff drink."

"Did his doctors put him on antidepressants when they discharged him? Because those meds don't mix well with alcohol. *Are* you on meds, Mr. Shaver?"

"They gave me some pills to take home with me," Buzzy grumbled. "I flushed them right down the toilet."

"He looked as if he needed a drink," Beryl said defensively. The newsroom fell silent now. Or make that almost silent.

"Oh, no. . . ." Glynis gazed up at the ceiling with a horrified look on her face. "What's that *tapping* sound?"

"I'm just a small-town newspaperman, Madam First *Se-e*lectman," Buzzy answered sourly. "But it sure sounds like rain to me."

Glynis shook her head in disbelief. "I honestly don't know how this day can get any worse."

"Stay loose—it's still early," Des said. "So let me see if I've got this straight: Bob Paffin can vouch for the congressman's whereabouts at the time of the shooting, and vice versa, which means that neither one of you has an alibi. Delia Paffin was at the supermarket, which means she was also on her way to and from the supermarket and has no one to vouch for her whereabouts while she was. Beryl Fairchild was driving to and fro and has no one to vouch for her either. And how about you, Glynis? Where were you an hour ago?"

Glynis blinked at her. "Why, I was in my office at Town Hall. You know that."

"No, I don't know that, actually. I called you on your cell. You could have been anywhere."

"Well, yes, that's true," she allowed. "But I *was* in my office. If you don't believe me my secretary can . . . you don't think that *I* had anything to—"

"I don't know what to think," Des said, looking around at the group of old friends. "But I do know that all of you, along with two of your gang who are no longer with us, Chase Fair-child and Congressman Cahoon's ex-wife, Noelle, made up a story one warm spring night forty-seven years ago. And now that story has finally caught up with you. Bob? You knew your brother Lance was underneath Dorset Street. You've always known it. That's why you fought so hard against re-grading it when you were first selectman. Also why you fought to stay in office for so many years. Thirty-four of them to be exact." She looked at Buzzy Shaver. "That's why you attacked Glynis so viciously during the campaign. Demanding recount after recount when the tally went against you. Denouncing her regrading plan as evil and just plain un-American. Be-cause you knew Lance was down there, too. *And* because you were doing Bob's bidding. He's been quietly bankrolling *The Gazette* for years. You would have folded a long time ago with-out his backing." On Buzzy's surprised look she said, "Yeah, I know all about that. Bart told me."

Again, the newsroom fell silent—aside from the hard, steady rain that was now falling on the roof.

"Two people are dead," Des went on. "One died in 1967. The other is still warm up at the Cahoon cemetery. You folks have been sitting on this story for your entire adult lives. It's time to get it out in the open. Tell me, what really happened to Lance that night?"

Not one of them would answer her. Or look at her or each other. They just stared straight ahead in stony silence.

"Tell her, Mother," Glynis said pleadingly. "Tell *me*."

Beryl Fairchild drew in her breath, but she remained mute.

Delia Paffin's head was starting to jiggle slightly on her neck. The lady was trembling with fear. And Bob Paffin, he of the weak heart, was looking real pale standing there next to her.

"You're not going to pass out on me again, are you?" Des asked him.

"Perhaps we should talk to an attorney," he responded weakly.

"I'm an attorney," Glynis reminded him.

"As am I, it so happens," the congressman said.

"Look, it's *over*, people," Des informed them. "You've held together for all of these years but it's *over*. A pair of top-notch Major Crime Squad investigators are going to be walking through that door any minute now. Either you can tell me *right now* what you've been hiding or you can tell them—in an interrogation room while the whole lot of you are under arrest for criminal conspiracy and illegal disposition of a body, just for starters. They will cut you *no* slack. Not even you, Congressman. You'll get no free pass."

"Wouldn't expect one," he said, his jaw clenched tight.

"I'm your resident trooper. If you're straight with me I'll do everything I can to help you out. I look out for my people. But once Lieutenant Snipes and Sergeant Tedone are here it'll be their case and I won't be able to do a thing for you. And I sure would feel a whole lot better if you'd give me that gun," she said to Buzzy Shaver. "Hand it over."

"No," he growled, gripping it tightly.

"You should have taken Bart's phone, too, you know."

He frowned at her. "His what?"

"His cell phone. After you shot him you took his laptop and notepads but you left his cell phone. I found it in the grass next to his body."

"I don't know what you're talking about."

"Bart's call log, Mr. Shaver. He placed two calls shortly before he died. One of them was to this office. He asked you to meet him up there, didn't he?"

"I *don't* know what you're talking about," he repeated.

"Sure, you do. I'm talking about your young cousin. The one who called you Uncle Buzzy as a sign of his affection. You were the only family he had. He loved you. He also loved *The Gazette*. Wanted to keep it going as an online newspaper. Build a life here for himself and his girlfriend, Mary Ann. The one you don't like because she's plain faced. She doesn't know yet that Bart's dead. I still have to call her and give her the news. I'm really looking forward to it." She moved a few steps closer to Buzzy, holding her hand out. "Give me the gun."

"No!" he snarled, baring his hideous yellow teeth at her.

"Give it to me. *Deal* with me. This is your last chance. Let me help you before it's too late."

Buzzy let out a wet, painful cough that wracked his entire chest. "You get away from me," he warned her, gasping for breath. "Get away or I'll shoot you right where you stand."

That was when the door to *The Gazette* opened.

But it wasn't Yolie and Toni who walked in.

CHAPTER 14

THE NEWSROOM WAS SO crowded with people that Mitch felt as if he'd just walked into a color-drenched remake of *Front Page Woman*, a zippy little 1935 Warner Brothers newsroom drama helmed by Michael Curtiz. All that was missing were Bette Davis, George Brent and the zippy. There was no zippy. The air was heavy with tension. And the place was teeming with public officials, past and present. US Congressman Luke Cahoon was standing there with his shaggy eyebrows and air of patrician authority. So was Glynis Fairchild-Forniaux, Dorset's hard-charging first selectwoman, along with Bob Paffin, her weak-chinned, snowy-haired dick of a predecessor and Bob's pudgy wife, Delia, with her rosy apple cheeks and Tang-colored hair. Beryl Fairchild, the first selectwoman's elegant, silver-haired mother was there. And Buzzy Shaver was slumped there in a chair at his rolltop desk with his liverish lower lip stuck out and a short-barreled revolver clutched in his right hand. He wasn't pointing it at anyone. But it had a way of commanding attention.

It sure had the attention of Dorset's uncommonly lovely resident trooper.

"Good afternoon, Master Sergeant," Mitch said to her.

Des peered at him in that way she did whenever she was worried about him. He did happen to be soaking wet—it was a long walk back to his truck in the rain. And he suspected that he still looked somewhat shaken, possibly because he was. "Right back at you," she said guardedly, glancing at the manila envelope that was tucked under his arm. "What have you got there?"

"A pretty darned good local news story for *The Gazette*. It's got political intrigue, suicide, sex, more sex. Oh, and a couple of murders, too."

"Young man, we're rather busy right now," the congressman said.

"On the contrary," Des said. "The door to *The Gazette* is always open. Anyone who has a story to share can just walk right in and share it. That's a Shaver family tradition, right?"

Buzzy Shaver didn't respond. Just sat there at his desk, gun in hand, glowering and wheezing.

Mitch noticed that he had a bottle of Old Overholt on the desk. "I *knew* you'd keep a bottle of Old Overalls around this place," he exclaimed. "Why, it's been the beloved house grog of ink-stained wretches from coast to coast ever since there have been ink-stained wretches from coast to coast. I used to work with an old-time restaurant critic who drank an *entire* bottle of that rotgut every single day. Really, really made me wonder what it was doing to her palate. Do you mind if I join you, Mr. Shaver?" There was a coffeemaker on a table over in the corner. Mitch fetched a Styrofoam cup and poured himself a generous jolt of the rye whiskey. "You're supposed to get plastered at a wake, right? That's what this is, isn't it? Mind you, I don't usually imbibe so early in the day. Especially the hard stuff. This is making me feel just like Jack Nicholson." He raised the Styrofoam cup ceremoniously into the air and drawled, "'Here's to the first of the day, fellas. To old D.H. Lawrence. . . .'" Mitch drank it down in one big gulp. As he felt it burn his throat he flapped his left elbow like a chicken and gasped, "'Nick-nick-nick, fiff-fiff-fiff, gyahh . . . *Indians.*'"

Everyone in the newsroom with the exception of Des stared at him in dumfounded amazement.

"Not a lot of *Easy Rider* fans here, huh? Why am I not surprised?" He poured himself another stiff jolt of the stuff. "Wow, this would remove that stubborn old varnish from my dining table in no time. I wonder what it's doing to the lining of my stomach. Check that, no I don't. Anyone else care to join me?" On their stony silence he said, "You keep this in your bottom desk drawer, am I right, Mr. Shaver? Sure I am. I knew that. But the gun's a bit of a surprise. Then again, I guess I shouldn't be surprised—considering the condition I found Bart in less than fifteen minutes after he called me."

"He called *you*?" Glynis spoke up.

Des said, "As I mentioned, Bart placed two calls shortly before he died. One was to his Uncle Buzzy. The other was to Mitch."

"Correct." Mitch gulped down his second shot of rye, aware of Des's gaze on him. "He asked me to meet him at the old Cahoon cemetery. The one that's right next to your house at the top of Johnny Cake Hill, Congressman."

The congressman said nothing to that. Just stared at him.

"But why did he call *you*?" Glynis wondered.

"Bart was doing a favor for me—speaking to someone on my behalf. I've just spoken to that someone and he confirmed that he did indeed talk to Bart shortly before Bart called me."

"Who were you speaking with?" Bob Paffin asked hoarsely.

"Young Henry, the head groundskeeper at the country club. I just love Dorset, don't you? Where else but hee-yah would a guy who's seventy-eight years old be called *Young* Henry? Nice fellow. Serves one heck of a bottle of Coca-Cola, too. A glass bottle, not plastic. Glass makes all of the difference." He glanced over at Des and said, "How am I doing so far, thin person?"

She smiled at him with her pale green eyes. "You're doing just fine."

"Thanks, don't mind if I do." He tossed back some more Old Overholt. "Did I remember to offer you a drink?"

"Thanks, but I'm on the clock right now. Mitch, what's in that envelope?"

"What, this? It's an eight-by-ten glossy of a wedding photo that ran in *The Gazette* back in 1969."

Buzzy Shaver stirred for the first time since Mitch had walked in. "Where'd you get that?" he demanded.

"From your files. Bart loaned it to me."

"He had no right to do that."

"And yet he did. How about that?" Mitch removed the photo from the envelope and set it on a desk for the others to look at. They crowded around him—all except for Buzzy, who sat stubbornly at his desk, gun in hand. "This will be a real trip down memory lane for you, Mr. and Mrs. Paffin. It's your wedding photo. You were married in the old rose garden at the club. You had to pull some strings because the garden was already booked for the date you wanted, but Chase Fairchild's father was president of the club and he made it happen. It must have been a lovely event. And yet you don't seem to have very fond memories of the old rose garden, Mrs. Paffin.

When I asked you a perfectly innocent question about it yesterday you got downright snappish. I couldn't imagine why. It got me to wondering, so I dropped by here and had a chat with Bart. Sure enough, *The Gazette* still had the photos of your big day. There's the two of you. . . ." Mitch tapped the photo with his index finger. "That's Chase Fairchild. That's you, Mrs. Fairchild. There's our future congressman, Luke Cahoon, with Noelle. There are Old Henry's roses. And, if you look closely, you'll notice the low wrought-iron spiked fence that used to enclose the garden. Or 'properly' enclose it, as you described it, Mrs. Paffin. It was removed after the fire of '92 destroyed the—"

"Pull over a sec," Des said. "Did you say *spiked* fence?"

"I did. I most certainly did."

She snatched the photo from the desk and had a closer look. "Keep talking."

"According to the ME, Lance Paffin suffered a fatal wound to the back of his skull from a tapered, spike-like object of some kind. Any number of objects could have made such a wound. My money was on a square-headed nail. My own cottage is full of them."

Congressman Cahoon shot a glare at Des. Mitch could only guess why.

"I wouldn't have given much consideration to the spiked fence around Old Henry's garden if Mrs. Paffin hadn't reacted the way that she did. When I asked Bart what might have happened to the fence he said he didn't know. But he did have a pretty good idea who would."

"Young Henry?" Des asked.

Mitch nodded. "Young Henry, who is Dorset through and

through. The man looks out for his neighbors and never throws a thing away. He maintains the Cahoon cemetery free of charge, you know. Some of the earliest brownstone gravestones up there have started to crumble. He was particularly concerned about a cluster of children's gravestones from way back in 1696. So he installed a protective fence around them. The very same fence that used to enclose Old Henry's rose garden. My guess? If you examine the spikes in that fence with the wound in the back of Lance Paffin's skull you'll find a match. My guess? Lance Paffin died right there at the club that night." He glanced over at Des and said, "Am I still doing okay?"

She smiled at him with her eyes again. "More than okay."

"Are you sure I can't offer you a drink?"

"Positive. Keep going."

"Thanks, don't mind if I do." Mitch poured himself another jolt of Old Overholt, turning his attention back to Buzzy Shaver. "After Bart spoke to Young Henry he called and asked me to meet him up there. That's why he called you, too. Bart was a good reporter. He didn't know why I was so interested in locating that particular fence. But he did know how to put two and two together and he figured it must have something to do with Lance's death. So he asked you about it, didn't he, Mr. Shaver? You were the natural person for him to ask. You know everything there is to know about this town's history. Unfortunately for Bart, you also know everything there is to know about what happened to Lance that night—because you took part in it. Poor Bart had no idea. And no way to know that when you drove up there you were planning to shoot him."

Buzzy stared down at the revolver in his hand. "He was a nosy damned pest."

"Nosy damned pests make the best reporters," Mitch informed him. "They taught us that in journalism school."

"Wouldn't take no for an answer. Kept fighting me over that same stupid story about Bob's driveway. The kid was a stubborn pain in the behind."

"Stubborn pains in the behind make the best reporters. They taught us that in journalism school, too."

"And then today he calls up and . . ." Buzzy trailed off, coughing wetly. "Tells me he has a pretty fair idea of how Lance died. Wants me to have a look up at the Cahoon cemetery before he goes public with it. So I headed up there."

"And you shot him," Des said quietly.

"I had to," he insisted, gazing around the newsroom. "I love these people. And they still have a lot of good years left. All I've got is a few months. I did it for the old bunch. They're like family to me."

"Yeah, but Bart *was* family," Mitch pointed out.

"And he was trying to destroy this newspaper," Buzzy said angrily. "Every single goddamned day he'd start in on how we were no longer a 'sustainable business model.' I told him *The Gazette* isn't a business—it's an institution. And I'll be damned if it disappears inside of some lousy computer on my watch."

"He asked you to meet him at the cemetery," Des said, nudging him along.

Buzzy nodded. "And he showed me that spiked fence. Told me he was positive it had something to do with Lance's death. I said, 'What do you know about Lance's death?' He said 'Not as much as you do.' I demanded to know what he meant by that. He said, 'You know what really happened. That's why you fought the regrading plan so hard. You and Bob both.' I told him to leave it alone. 'It's ancient history,' I said to him. 'Let the dead stay dead.' Do you know what that kid said to me? He said, 'No, sir, this is one story you are *not* going to bury.' He wouldn't listen to me. Wouldn't goddamned listen. Just started to walk away. So I stopped him," Buzzy said, hefting the gun in his hand.

"Three shots to the back make for a very effective stopper," Mitch acknowledged. "But you didn't finish the job, Mr. Shaver. You also needed to kill Young Henry, who knows where that fence is, and you needed to kill me before I had a chance to show this photo to our resident trooper. But you're not much of a pro at this murder thing, are you?" He drank down some more of Buzzy Shaver's Old Overholt, smacking his lips with pleasure. He was actually starting to like the taste of the stuff. What was *that* about? "Master Sergeant, would you like to hear something totally whack?"

"You trying to tell me that what I've been listening to isn't whack?"

"If they'd just called the police and said it was an accident they would have gotten away with it. Lance was a high-spirited, reckless sort. He got plastered, slipped and hit his head on the fence. Bam. It happens. Stuff like that happens. There would have been a lot of tut-tutting about rich kids who drink too much but absolutely no one would have gone to jail. They didn't do that. They went all John Ford instead."

Des frowned at him. "They went all what?"

"They circled the wagons to protect one of their own."

"Who?"

"Whoever Lance was fighting with when he smacked his head on the spiked fence."

"Before you say another word, young fellow, I'd like to remind you that this gun holds six bullets." Buzzy raised it and pointed it right at Mitch. "I fired three. That means I've still got three."

Mitch's mouth suddenly went dry. He really, really didn't like having guns pointed at him—especially when they weren't loaded with movie blanks. He was a total wuss that way.

"I could shoot both you and the resident trooper right here and now before the major crime folks arrive. That'll nip this thing right in the bud."

"I'm afraid it won't, Mr. Shaver," Des responded in a voice that Mitch found remarkably calm. Not that it surprised him. His ladylove's coolness in the face of danger never surprised him. Ice water. She had ice water in her veins. "Lieutenant Snipes and Sergeant Tedone already know everything that I know. Besides, Mitch and I aren't standing right next to you the way Bart was. We must be a good ten feet away."

Mitch gauged the distance with his eyes. "More like twelve feet."

She shook her head. "Looks like ten to me."

"Twelve. Want me to pace it off?"

"Not necessary."

"It'll only take a sec. Are you sure?"

"Quite sure." She turned back to Buzzy. "You're elderly and a bit on the shaky side. I'm young and fast on the draw. I also have way more firepower than you do. This is a SIG-Sauer P229 .40 caliber semiautomatic weapon that I'm carrying.

Since I happen to be the one who's armed you'll shoot me first. I'm betting my life it won't be a kill shot. I doubt you'll even hit me at all from where you're sitting. Even if you do I'll still shoot that Ruger right out of your hand and that will be the end of it. So do yourself a favor and drop it, Mr. Shaver, okay? Drop your damned gun *now*!"

CHAPTER 15

"Time out, what if his first shot hits *me*?"

"It won't," Des assured Mitch, her eyes never leaving Buzzy's raised gun. "I'm the one who's armed, remember?"

"Yeah, but he might aim at you and hit me instead. He's old and shaky, remember?"

"Mitch, that's not going to happen," she said, really, really hoping her voice sounded steady and calm. Because she wasn't feeling steady or calm. She was genuinely terrified that this wheezing wretch of an old man was going to shoot the man she loved.

"But how can you be so sure?" Mitch's own voice sounding a bit thick. He'd downed, what, three doubles in less than thirty minutes? Not like him at all. He was trying to numb his grief. And yet, somehow, he was still managing to fit all of the pieces together in a way that made an amazing amount of sense. Des didn't know how he did it. Whether it was because of the thousands of movie plots he had tucked away in his size-genius brain or if he was just remarkably intuitive. But her wow man had a gift, no getting around it.

"I do this for a living, okay?" she said to him patiently. "And I need for you to shut up a second. And Mr. Shaver, I need for you to give it up. There is no way you're going to take out both of us before I blow a big hole through your gun hand."

"You'll have to kill me, too, Buzzy," Glynis warned him. "I won't watch you murder two people and keep quiet. I'm an officer of the court. I've taken an oath to uphold the law, and I will. So will Congressman Cahoon." On Luke Cahoon's rather startled look she said, "Won't you, Congressman?"

Luke Cahoon gazed at Dorset's first selectwoman reflectively. "I don't believe I want to find out the answer to that question. Buzzy, mind if I have a drink of your rotgut?"

"*Now* it's turning into a party," Mitch exclaimed happily.

"Help yourself, Luke." Buzzy fished another shot glass from the bottom desk drawer with his left hand, his right still clutching the Ruger. "And pour me one while you're at it."

Luke Cahoon filled both shot glasses and held Buzzy's out to him. When Buzzy reached for it the congressman snatched the Ruger from his other hand.

"Luke, what are you doing?"

"The right thing." He held it out to Des by its short barrel. "The sane thing."

She took it from him, pocketing it. "Thank you, Congressman."

"Don't thank me," he said coldly. "I didn't do it for you."

Buzzy glowered at Luke, his chest rising and falling with great difficulty. Every breath he took sounded like a wet, torn bellows.

"We've gotten off of the subject here," Glynis stated firmly, her eyes locking on to Beryl's. "*You* were there that night, Mother. All of you were there. And you can't keep this a secret any longer. So why don't you just tell us what really happened to Lance?"

The old friends maintained their guilty silence. Wouldn't so much as look at each other.

Until Buzzy finally spoke up. "You want to know what really happened?" he blustered. "Fine, I'll tell you. When I heard that he'd dared to show his face at the club I let the smug bastard have it, okay? Because he did not belong around decent people. Not after what he'd done to Frances. He *killed* her. So I killed him." Buzzy held his wrists out to Des. "Get your handcuffs out. It's me who you want. I killed Lance. And I'm not sorry. I've never been sorry."

Des considered his confession carefully. "How did you hear that Lance had dared to show his face at the club? I was told that you didn't attend the dance. Had to stay home with your mother."

Buzzy peered at her balefully. "I knew a kid who bussed tables there. He called me from the kitchen and told me, okay? What happened to Frances, that was something Mother never got over. Frances was a treasure. And that bastard, he wiped his feet on her. I-I got in my car and drove over there. Told Lance to step out into the parking lot. When we got outside I told him he had no business associating with decent people and to get the hell out of Dorset. Go fly his jet planes. Fly one into the side of a mountain somewhere for all I cared. The bastard just laughed at me and called me a name I won't repeat in front of ladies. So I punched him. Caught him off guard, I guess. He tumbled over backwards and cracked his skull against that spiked fence that was around the garden. One minute he was standing there laughing at me. The next minute he was lying there dead." Buzzy drank down his shot glass full of rye. "The other fellows wanted to call the police. But if we'd done that then the girls would have gotten dragged into it simply for being there. I didn't want their reputations to suffer because of that bastard. It was bad enough that Frances gave up her own life for him. Luke was sympathetic to that."

"And Bob, too?" Des glanced over at Dorset's former first selectman. "He helped you cover up his own brother's death as an act of, what, chivalry?"

"Absolutely," Buzzy replied.

Des glanced over at Delia Paffin and Beryl Fairchild, whose eyes remained fastened on the floor. Then she turned to Mitch and said, "I'm not buying this, are you?"

"Not so much. But I've had quite a bit to drink."

"I haven't."

"It's the truth, damn it," Buzzy insisted. "We sent Delia, Beryl and Noelle home, then stuffed Lance in the trunk of his Mustang and drove him to Dorset Street. The town was planning to repave it on Monday. I figured if we dug a hole and covered him over no one would ever know what happened."

"And what about shipwrecking the *Monster*?" Des asked him.

"My idea, too," he answered quickly, wetting his lower lip with a dart of his grayish tongue. "It was an entirely believable way for a hot dog like Lance to go. And with the Connecticut River's current it was also believable that his body wouldn't turn up. Luke and I took the *Monster* out. Chase followed us in the little runabout that the Fairchilds kept at the yacht club. Bob stayed behind on lookout, but no one happened by. First thing Monday morning public works repaved Dorset Street and as far as the world was concerned Lance disappeared at sea."

"What did you do with Lance's wallet?"

"We dumped it overboard."

"Yet you didn't remove his class ring or his Rolex. Why not?"

"Because that would have been disrespectful."

Des turned to Mitch and said, "I'm still not buying this, are you?"

"Not so much. But I've had quite a bit to drink."

"I haven't."

"When I got back here from the cemetery," Buzzy went on, "I was planning to use this pistol on myself. Finish the job I didn't have the nerve to do yesterday at my shack. But I couldn't get Beryl to leave. She's very determined, in her own quiet way." Again, he held his wrists out to Des. "You've got me. Take me away."

"Very well, Mr. Shaver." Des reached ever so slowly for the handcuffs on her Sam Browne belt. "If that's how you want it."

"Wait, Buzzy, I can't let you do this!" Bob Paffin blurted out.

"Shut up," Buzzy growled at him.

"But it's not right!"

"I agree with Bob on this, Buzzy," Luke Cahoon said. "It's not right."

"*I'm* the one who you want," Bob confessed, his voice quavering. "*I* punched Lance. We got into a dumb fight about kid stuff. Stupid kid stuff. He was teasing me about the way I used to stammer when I was a little boy. Started calling me

B-B-Bombo again. That's what he used to call me. Little B-B-Bombo. God, I hated that nickname. And Lance knew it. So he kept taunting me, just like he did when we were boys. He could be very cruel."

"And yet you idolized him," Des pointed out.

"*Idolized* him?" Bob let out a humorless laugh. "Not a chance. I *hated* him. My brother was a vicious bully. He tormented me beyond belief when I was little. I was afraid of small spaces, and Lance knew that. When I was seven he locked me in a storage cupboard down in the basement and wouldn't let me out for hours. I sobbed and sobbed and eventually peed all over myself. He laughed. He thought it was hilarious. When I was ten he wrapped me up with masking tape and locked me in my closet for half of the night while he and a neighbor girl had sex in his bedroom. I peed all over myself then, too."

"I'm beginning to sense a recurring theme here," Mitch observed.

"Humiliation," Bob said bitterly. "You know what I used to call him? 'The King.' We all did, with sneers on our faces, because he thought the simple, basic rules of human decency, the ones that the rest of us live by, didn't apply to him. That night of the spring dance he pushed me too far. And I-I finally fought back. And you know the rest." He held his wrists out to her. "You know everything now."

Des let out a sigh of regret. "Well, I tried. I was really hoping to spare you folks the indignity, but I'm afraid we'll have to take all of you in for questioning when the Major Crime Squad gets here." She started counting heads. "I do believe we're going to need two cars."

"But why?" Bob protested. "I've just told you what happened."

"And I know that you're lying," Des said. "Here's what I think. I think you good folks made up a story about what happened that warm spring night and you've stuck to it like the good, loyal friends you are—right down to the smallest detail like 'stoked.' How many times did I hear you say Lance was 'stoked' for a sail? But you never had a plan for what you'd do when Lance's body was finally found, did you? All you could hope to do was run out the clock. Chase Fairchild got lucky. He didn't have to face this day. Nor did the congressman's ex-wife, Noelle. But the rest of you are still here. And now you have to deal with it. It's taken forty-seven years but the truth has finally caught up with you."

"We've made a difference," Luke Cahoon pointed out. "Led useful lives. There's justice in that. And justice in what happened to him. Lance Paffin was a predator who didn't deserve to live."

"So, what, you folks executed him?"

"I punched him," Bob repeated insistently. "I punched him and he hit his head on the fence."

She glanced over at Mitch. "I'm still not buying it, are you?"

"Not so much."

"What are you thinking?"

"That Lance's wicked, wicked way with women got him killed. It's a pretty long list of women. Longer than we realized. Young Henry just added a new name to it."

"Really? Do tell."

"It seems that back in '62, when the gang was still in high school, Lance had a torrid fling with one of their mothers—a shmokin' blonde who was in her early forties at the time. Young Henry stumbled upon the two of them together by the club pool one morning, stark naked. He never told a soul about it. He was afraid that the pretty blonde would get him fired. Babette Fairchild was in a position to get him fired. Her husband, Chase's father, was president of the country club at the time."

Glynis whirled and gaped at her mother in horror. "Lance Paffin slept with *Nana Baba*?"

Beryl didn't answer her. Just stood there in mortified silence.

"Chase must have found out. I can't imagine Lance didn't boast about it," Mitch said. "How could he resist? He nailed the guy coming and going."

"What is that supposed to mean?" Glynis demanded.

"It means," Beryl said, "that I had to arrange a special trip to Barbados during my senior year at Wellesley because of Lance."

"He got you *pregnant*?"

Beryl lowered her gaze, coloring slightly. "Yes."

"Did father know?"

"Of course he knew," Mitch said. "Your father hated Lance Paffin."

Beryl stiffened. "How dare you accuse a man who's not here to defend himself. My husband was honorable and decent."

"I didn't say he wasn't. Just that he had a really good reason for wanting Lance dead. Same as Congressman Cahoon and Mr. Shaver and Lance's kid brother, Bob, who has conveniently neglected to mention that Lance also had his way with Delia."

"That's a damned lie!" Bob said indignantly.

"Nope, it's the damned truth. It's also the golden sombrero. *All* of you guys hated him for what he did to your women." Mitch helped himself to some more of Buzzy Shaver's Old Overholt. "How am I doing, Master Sergeant? Still okay?"

"More than okay."

He tilted his head at her curiously. "You sound surprised."

"Never. I'm in awe. Is there more?"

"A teeny-tiny bit more." He looked over at Delia Paffin, who stood there in grim silence next to Bob. She'd started to shake, as if the earth were quaking under her feet.

Mitch stared at her, his gaze steady and unblinking. Des had never seen her man's eyes bore into anyone quite so intensely before.

Delia gazed back at him, then looked away. Or tried to. Her own eyes kept returning to him, as if she were powerless to stop them. "Why do you keep looking at me that way?" she demanded.

"How did it feel?"

"How did *what* feel?"

"Getting caught that way."

"Young man, I have no idea what you are talking about," she answered contemptuously. "Do you?"

"Yeah, I do. I most certainly do. I'm told that you had quite a frisky reputation back in your day, Mrs. Paffin. No disrespect intended. Believe me, I sowed plenty of wild oats myself. Well, no, I didn't. Mostly, I sat by myself in darkened movie houses eating pastrami sandwiches and kosher dill pickles. *Never* got laid. But that's a whole other plot. Your nickname around Dorset was Easy Deezy. Everybody knew it. Everybody except for your beloved Bob."

"Now you j-just hold on there!" Bob sputtered at him angrily.

"I repeat, how did it feel when Bob caught the two of you together that night? You were on one of those teak benches in Old Henry's garden, weren't you? That's why you got so snarly with me yesterday when I asked you about them. Sure, you and Lance were tucked into a nice, quiet corner of the rose garden getting busy when your beloved Bob caught you in the act. He found out. *That's* what really happened, isn't it?"

The newsroom fell silent again, aside from the rain that was coming down hard on the roof.

"Yes, that's what really happened," Bob conceded in a heavy voice. "I caught them there together. And instead of apologizing to me Lance *bragged* about how Delia couldn't get enough of him. A tramp. That's what he called her, among other things, while she was sitting right there before us." He looked at Des pleadingly. "I was hoping to keep her name out of this. You can understand that, can't you? But everything else I just told you is true. I ordered him to stand up on his two feet like a man. When he did I popped him one and he hit his head on that fence. You know the rest. That's it. That's the whole—"

"*Stop* this, Bob!" Delia cried out suddenly. "For God's sake, *please* stop, will you?"

Bob placed a bony hand on her shoulder. "Let me handle it. Everything's going to be fine."

"No, everything's *not* going to be fine! I can't *stand* it any longer!" Delia began to sob. Huge, wrenching sobs. Her chest was heaving. Tears streamed down her chubby cheeks. "I won't let you do this. I won't! My God, Buzzy, you actually *killed* Bart—a sweet young boy who had his whole life ahead of him. How am I supposed to look at myself in the mirror? Tell me how!"

Buzzy didn't tell her anything. Just sat there in defeated silence.

"You're upset, dear," Bob said soothingly. "We're all upset. It's been a rough couple of days. But you need to calm down."

"Bob's right, Delia," Luke Cahoon said. "You don't want to say anything to these people that you'll regret, do you?"

"Let her speak," Beryl said to them in a firm voice.

Bob blinked at her, startled. "Excuse me?"

"Delia has been carrying this around for too long," she told him. "So have I. And I will not stand here and silently countenance the murder of that young man."

Glynis reached over and held her mother's hand tightly in hers.

Delia found a tissue in her purse and dabbed at her eyes, sniffling. "Will someone please give me a drink?"

"Don't mind if I do." Mitch fetched her the shot glass of Old Overholt that Buzzy had filled for the congressman.

Delia drank it down, shuddering. "I'm the one who killed Lance." Her voice was low and flat now. She had no more emotion left inside of her. "Not Bob. Not Buzzy. It was me. The four of them took care of his body to protect me. In our day the men were supposed to look out for us. And they looked out for me.

"I'd bought a new gown for the dance," she recalled. "And I'd been starving myself for a week so I'd fit into it. The champagne went right to my head. And we drank *buckets* of it. Lance

217

had to go back to that awful war in the morning. He didn't want the night to end. None of us did. We were all so giddy. God knows I certainly was. It was such a wonderful night."

"Even though Lance and Luke argued in the parking lot over Noelle?" Des asked.

"That was just Lance being Lance," Delia said mildly. "I understood that about him. We all did. Didn't we, Beryl?"

"Yes," Beryl said, her blue eyes shining.

"Not long after he and Luke quarreled," she went on, "Lance pulled me aside and told me he wanted me—right that very minute. It never even occurred to me to say no to him. I was high as a kite. And I adored him. He was exciting, confident, fun. . . ."

"Everything I wasn't," Bob said miserably.

"I excused myself and toddled off to the ladies' room. Lance slipped away and joined me in Old Henry's garden. We'd done that at least a dozen times before and dear Bob never noticed. Never so much as suspected a thing." Delia's face fell. "But that night he . . ."

"I was feeling queasy from all of that champagne," Bob explained. "It isn't just the sea that riles my stomach. I don't do well with sweet wine. Or fatty meat. And the prime rib that night had definitely been on the fatty side. I could feel it churning away in my—"

"Really don't need to hear this part," Mitch assured him.

"I stepped out into the garden for a breath of air and found them together on a bench."

"It could not have been more awful," Delia remembered, her voice hushed. "Lance's pants were unzipped, my head was in his lap. Do I need to draw you a picture?"

"I think you just did," Mitch assured her.

"I can never, ever forget the look on poor Bob's face when he caught us there. Until that moment he'd thought I was as pure as the driven snow. He hadn't known a thing about Lance or the others. And there were others. Not that many, but a few. They wanted me. I liked to be wanted. I liked to make men happy. Bob was very traditional. He wanted me to be a certain type of girl and so for Bob I became that girl. I liked being that girl." Delia smiled at him sadly. "I still do."

"What happened when he caught the two of you?" Des asked her.

"It was just as Bob said. Lance became incredibly abusive. He said, 'Didn't you know, B-B-Bombo? Your b-b-beloved Delia will b-b-blow anyone.' Bob ordered him to stand up and take what was coming to him. They began to scuffle there in the garden, Bob throwing wild punches, Lance laughing at him and taunting him. By now the others—Beryl, Chase, Luke and Noelle—had heard them yelling and joined us out there. It wasn't much of a fight. Lance was so much bigger than Bob, and had been trained in hand-to-hand combat. He could have killed Bob if he'd wanted to. But he just let him have it once in the stomach, hard, and had himself a good laugh watching Bob puke his prime rib dinner all over Old Henry's ornamental flowering—"

"Really don't need to hear this part either," Mitch assured her.

"He laughed and laughed. That was when I decided I'd had just about enough of Lance Paffin. I told him so to his face. And then I shoved him. He wasn't expecting me to do that. I sent him teetering backward. He pitched over and cracked his skull on that spiked fence, twitched a couple of times and was dead. I killed him. It was an accident. But everything we did after that wasn't. We should have called the police. We didn't. Instead, we—we . . ."

"We protected our fort," Bob explained. "Same as we'd been doing since we played cowboys and Indians together behind Buzzy's house on Appleby Lane." He smiled faintly at the childhood recollection. "Remember that old fort of yours, Buzzy?"

"Guess you haven't been out back in a while," Buzzy responded. "It's still there. Couldn't bring myself to tear it down. A family of raccoons took up residence there last winter."

"We used to call ourselves the Appleby Gang. Chase was always our idea man. Smarter than all of the rest of us put together." Bob's face tightened. "He knew exactly what to do that night."

Glynis glared at him accusingly. "Are you saying it was my father's idea to bury Lance underneath Dorset Street?"

Bob nodded his head. "And to wreck the *Monster*. I'm sorry, but that's the truth, Glynis. Chase was the brains of the Appleby Gang. Luke was our leader. Always the calmest under fire. He put the girls in Beryl's car and sent them straight home while I called Buzzy from the pay phone by the pool. I told Buzzy to grab every shovel he could find and meet us in front of the Congregational Church." Bob smiled at his old friend. "I knew we could count on Buzzy. There's no one more loyal."

"Chase's plan worked to perfection," Des said. "Except for the fingerprint evidence that the techies took from the tiller of the *Monster*. Nice, fresh fingerprints that would have shown you'd recently piloted Lance's boat, Congressman."

"You're right, they would have," Luke Cahoon acknowledged. "But Dave Stank, the lead investigator, was hungry to get somewhere. He took care of the fingerprint evidence, and I took care of him. Things worked out just fine."

Delia Paffin gazed at her husband affectionately. "And Bob forgave me for being such a silly girl. We've raised our children, grown old together and we've been very happy, haven't we?"

"Yes, we have," Bob assured her, his voice soaring with conviction.

Des didn't know if she believed him or not. And she definitely wondered if Delia did. But he had stayed by Delia's side for all of these years and guarded her secret and that did say something about Bob Paffin as a man, even if Des still thought he was a consummate weasel.

"Why didn't you stop me, Mother?" Glynis wondered aloud. "Why did you let me go charging ahead with my road project?"

"I didn't want you getting mixed up in it," Beryl answered. "It wasn't your secret. It was ours."

Mitch drank down the last of his Old Overholt, shaking his head. "I'm not wired like you people are. I couldn't live with such a huge lie for so many years."

"We did what needed doing," Luke Cahoon said loftily. "It was our duty."

"For the first year I had to avoid that intersection entirely," Delia confessed. "I couldn't drive over him. Just couldn't. I-I did learn to live with it. But the horror has never, ever gone away. Not once have I forgotten that Lance was down there in that coal black asphalt tomb. I still have nightmares that he's trying to claw his way up through the pavement. He was like a naughty little boy, you know. And he's remained that little boy. He never changed. Never got older. Not like the rest of us." She took a ragged breath, letting it out slowly. "I'm relieved that this is finally out in the open. I'm glad that you found him."

"I'm glad that you're glad," Des said to her. "It's a shame that Bart can't be here to share in this moment."

Delia Paffin recoiled as if Des had just slapped her in the face. Possibly because she had.

Now was when Yolie and Toni walked in the door, both of them wearing rain-soaked slickers.

"What have you got for us, girl?" Yolie asked Des, her eyes flicking around the newsroom at everyone.

"Bart's shooter is seated at the desk. Say hello to Mr. Clyde 'Buzzy' Shaver. I've got the murder weapon right here," Des said, patting her jacket pocket. "Lance Paffin's death was accidental. Mrs. Paffin shoved him and he hit his head. The others then buried his body under Dorset Street and staged his disappearance at sea. We're talking involuntary manslaughter, criminal conspiracy and illegal disposition of a body. And the statute of limitations ran out on all of those charges after, what, seven years? But the district prosecutor will have to sort that out once these folks make their formal statements. They're all yours, Yolie. Except for the first selectwoman. She was just here to observe."

Yolie looked at Des in astonishment. "Are you saying we're all done?"

"What I'm saying. You'll need transportation for everyone in this room who's over the age of seventy."

Toni cleared her throat. "Including the congressman? . . ."

"She said *everyone*," Yolie barked.

"On it, Loo." Toni reached for her cell.

Mitch watched Toni as she phoned it in, gazing at her curiously.

Yolie smiled at him. "Hey, sweet thing. How are you?"

"Quite hammered," he stated with solemn gravity. "I am going to have one mondo headache in the morning."

"Mitch is blaming himself for Bart's death," Des explained.

Yolie stuck her chin out at him. "Did you pull the trigger?"

"No, I did not."

"Then don't beat yourself up over what some other fool did," she blustered. "You'll make yourself crazy. Are you hearing me or do I have to slug you?"

"I'm hearing you."

"Good." Yolie kissed him on the cheek and said, "Damn, I love me the sensitive type." Then she placed Buzzy Shaver under arrest for Bart's murder.

Des took Mitch's hand and brushed it with her lips. "How did you know?"

"How did I know what?"

"That it was Delia."

"Didn't you notice the way she was shaking? Her hooters were jiggling just like Arlene Dahl's when the earth's core erupted at the end of *Journey to the Center of the Earth*. Great sequence, by the way. All except for the part when Count Saknussem ate Gertrude the duck. That was totally unacceptable."

"Doughboy, do you realize that sometimes I have *no* idea what you're talking about?"

"But sometimes you do. That's pretty cool, isn't it?"

"It's very cool."

"Girl, I owe you one," Yolie said as she steered Buzzy Shaver toward the door. The old newspaperman seemed very calm. Almost serene. Des wondered if he, too, was relieved the secret was finally out. "Word, I'll make it up to you next time."

"There's going to be a next time?"

Yolie let out a laugh. "Hell, yeah. This is the thin white edge of paradise, remember?"

Toni ushered the rest of the old bunch out the door while Glynis remained there in the middle of the newsroom with a stricken expression on her face. Dorset's first selectwoman looked as if her entire world had come crashing down around her. Possibly because it had.

"Am I seeing things or is Toni sporting an engagement ring?" Mitch asked Des.

"A promise ring, actually. I'll tell you about it later."

"Who's the lucky guy?"

"I'll *tell* you about it later. Right now, I think I'd better give you a ride home."

"Yeah, I think you'd better, too. I'm feeling kind of sleepy all of a sudden. Hey, Des?"

"Yes?"

"Let's not have prime rib for dinner tonight, okay?"

"Okay. You talked me into it."

"Hey, Des?"

"*Yes?*"

"Bart was right," he said, sniffing at the air. "You *can* still smell the ink in here on damp days."

Des couldn't smell a thing, but she didn't see any point in telling him that. So she didn't.

Epilogue

(ONE WEEK LATER)

THE WEATHER FORECAST WAS more than just a little bit off. Those showers that began to fall on the day Bart Shaver died developed into powerful thunderstorms in the night. According to the National Weather Service, nearly three inches of rain fell on Dorset in a period of less than two hours. An additional five inches of hard, steady rain fell the following day, transforming Dorset Street from a dirt road into a rushing river that roiled its muddy way through the entire historic district. Homes, businesses and Town Hall were flooded. Des had to evacuate several elderly Dorset Street residents by carrying them from their front porches out to the emergency motor launches that navigated the historic district for two days and nights. Schools were cancelled until the floodwaters receded four days later, leaving behind a sticky, oozy muck that stank of creosote. It was a total disaster for Dorset's new first selectwoman. The only way that Glynis's signature road project could have gone any worse was if the crew had found a dead body buried underneath the old pavement.

Oh, wait, they had.

Things did turn out okay once the roadbed had a chance to dry out. The Wilcox Paving crew returned and rerolled Dorset Street and the huge paving machine extruded fresh, smooth asphalt pavement that was plenty wide enough for a bike lane. The public works team laid sidewalks where there had previously been none. And the local TV news crews were there to film it when Sheila Enman personally oversaw the planting of three new copper beeches out in front of the Congregational Church. Good sized ones, too. Not itty-bitty saplings. Everyone seemed quite pleased with the way the project turned out, actually. Everyone except for the first selectwoman herself, who seemed to take no pleasure in its successful outcome. Or in anything else. Glynis was simply not the same lady after she'd found out what her own parents had been keeping secret for all of their adult lives.

The freakish unearthing of Lance Paffin's tomb became front-page news across America. There was no escaping the media spotlight. Not after Luke Cahoon resigned his congressional seat just as he'd promised he would. The scandal surrounding Lance's death sent shock waves through Dorset. Luke Cahoon was a hometown celebrity and hero. Bob Paffin had been first selectman for as long as most Dorseteers could remember, just as Buzzy Shaver had been the man who'd run *The Gazette*. Delia Paffin and Beryl Fairchild had led practically every worthy charitable organization in town. These people were Dorset's aristocracy. They'd epitomized everything that was fine and decent about the gem of Connecticut's Gold Coast. Now they were figures of shame and disgrace. They wouldn't go to jail for what they'd done on that warm spring night back in 1967. The statute of limitations had indeed run out long ago on their crimes. The law couldn't touch them. And Des doubted it could touch Buzzy, who'd been under psychiatric observation the day before he shot Bart. She felt certain that his attorney would successfully craft an insanity escape hatch. But there was no escaping what the unearthing of Lance Paffin had done to the close-knit village of Dorset. It made folks uneasy. Made them ask themselves if they, too, were capable of living with such a horrible secret for so long. Made them wonder who else in town was, and what other secrets lay hidden in Dorset's past just waiting to be dug up.

They wondered. Everyone wondered.

The Deacon phoned Des not long after the old bunch was taken into custody. "I guess you handled this as well as could be expected under the circumstances," he said to her somberly. Which was a rave review coming from the Deacon. This was not a man given to ego stroking. "Do you feel compromised now?"

"Compromised how, Daddy?"

"Would you like to be assigned somewhere else?"

"Hell, no. Dorset's my home. I've got skin in the game here. I'm not going anywhere else, hear me?"

"That's fine by me, Desiree. I just thought I'd ask."

Des had the unhappy task of phoning Bart Shaver's fiancée, Mary Ann Athey. Mary Ann took the news of his death with stoic reserve and made the drive to Dorset from Vassar to take charge of things. She turned out to be a rangy lacrosse player with a strong jaw and an admirably calm demeanor. Bart was buried at Duck River Cemetery three days after the ME released his body. Quite a few of their friends were in attendance. So were Des and Mitch. Mitch stood there stone-faced, holding Des's hand as Reverend Goode of the Congregational Church said whatever words of comfort anyone could possibly say. Mary Ann had arranged for coffee and cake in the church's community room afterward, but Mitch wasn't up for that. Instead, he wanted to go home and watch a DVD of *The Day the Earth Stood Still*—not the from-hunger remake with Keanu Reeves but the original 1951 black-and-white version with Michael Rennie and Patricia Neal. Des sat and watched the whole movie with him and found it reasonably enjoyable for an old sci-fi film. She had no idea why Mitch found it a comfort to watch it after Bart's funeral. There were many things about Mitch she didn't understand. He was, after all, a man. But he was her man.

He went to work on his new patio just as soon as the stormy weather allowed. Dug his way down a good six inches, then shoveled in a deep, level bed of stone dust before he positioned the heavy slabs of bluestone *just so* and tamped them into place with a rubber mallet, one by one by one. It was slow, hard physical work. It was exactly the sort of work Mitch needed to do right now.

He worked on the patio by himself in the chilly April sunshine. His usual helpmate, Bitsy Peck, was busy making sure that *The Gazette* continued to report the news of the day on its Web site. What with Bart gone and Buzzy under court-ordered psychiatric observation someone had to take over. That someone was the crusading one-time editor in chief of the Smith College *Sophian*, who leapt eagerly into the void and enlisted a half dozen of her equally eager lady friends to help out. Strange but true—Buzzy Shaver's all-male clubhouse had finally been taken over by the ladies whom he'd shut out for so many years. There was even talk that Bitsy, who had tons of Peck family money behind her, intended to buy *The Gazette*. Mitch took some comfort in knowing that Bart's death created a void that gave Bitsy a renewed purpose in life. And he felt certain she'd blossom in her new role. It did help a little. Just not enough.

He'd set almost a third of the patio stones in place when Des came *thumpety-thumping* across the old wooden causeway in her cruiser to get her first good look at it.

"Mitch, this is gorgeous," she exclaimed, standing there with her hands on her hips. "And I am loving the herringbone pattern. Did you design it?"

"Not exactly," he said softly as he knelt there in the stone dust.

Her face fell. "Oh. . . ."

"Are you okay with that?"

"Of course I am," she said quickly. "We are who we are. And who we *were*. We should embrace that. Nothing good comes from burying it. Just look what happens when you do."

"I'd rather not look if you don't mind. I keep seeing Bart lying there in the grass." He glanced up at her. "Don't you?"

She gazed out at the gentle swells on the sound. "Of course I do."

"But you draw your way out of it, is that it?"

"I used to draw my way out of it. These days I don't think there's a name for what I'm doing. Oh, wait, yes there is. It's called crap."

"Have you got your drawing pad in your trunk?"

"Always. Why?"

"Because she'll want to look at it."

She frowned at him suspiciously. "Who will?"

"Susan Vail, that professor from the art academy. She'll be here in . . ." He glanced at his watch. "Thirty-seven minutes. We have a drink date."

Her pale green eyes widened at him. "Who has a drink date?"

"You, me and Susan. I took matters into my own hands."

"Meaning what?" she demanded. "Did you two conversate about me?"

"Okay, now you're just trying to piss me off."

She stared at him in that the stiff-necked way of hers that never failed to remind him she was, and always would be, the Deacon's daughter. "Mitch, what did you say to her?"

"That your shit's fucked up."

"And what did she . . ."

"That you're the most gifted talent she's ever encountered and she'd be honored to work with you one-on-one."

"I *told* you I can't afford that."

"It's all taken care of. I'm giving some guest lectures at the academy on the subject of visual composition in the cin-e-ma. You know me—I can flap these receding gums for hours about Gregg Toland's deep-focus camera work in *Citizen Kane*. And the way Robert Siodmak lit the opening sequence of *The Killers*? Totally film noir meets Edward Hopper. Hell, I can go on for weeks."

"Are they paying you for these lectures?"

"Well, no."

"So you're volunteering your time?"

"Well, yeah."

She showed him her huge wraparound smile. "Have I told you recently that I adore you? Oh, hey, I almost forgot. . . ."

She reached into her jacket pocket and pulled out a fresh package of Stim-U-Dents. "For a job well done. I couldn't have cracked the Lance Paffin case without you."

"I think you'd have been better off without me on this one."

"And I think you couldn't be more wrong. I'm lost in the tall grass without you. Don't you know that?"

He hefted the Stim-U-Dents in his hand, peering at her. "I seem to recall that you hate these things."

"True that. And if I catch you chewing on one in public I'll make you eat it on the spot. But a man's got a right to do whatever he pleases when he's in the privacy of his own island."

Mitch tore open the package and stuck one in the corner of his mouth, chewing on it contentedly. "So anywhere on Big Sister is okay?"

"Anywhere on Big Sister. Anywhere at all." She gazed at him through her eyelashes. "Anywhere except for the sleeping loft."

Mitch gazed back at her, grinning. "I can live with that."